Born in Quebec City, Quebec, Canada, Laurie Le Roux always found herself at home among books and stories. After having completed her first writing at the age of nine, she decided to turn to different writing genres and styles. Her inspiration comes from the experiences she lived during her childhood and adolescence, to which she added a bit of imagination and fantasy. But the most important to her remains the following: writing stories that aren't only meant to be read, but also to be lived.

To a dear friend of mine –
I hope the book will be like a ray of sunshine to you.

To Miroslaw,

My time in Newcastle was one of the greatest.
I'm glad we have met
And hope the book will, to you, be as great;
a reminder of that sept.dec 2023 semester ✨

Laurie LeRao

8.12.2023

Laurie Le Roux

HEARTLESS

Austin Macauley Publishers™
LONDON · CAMBRIDGE · NEW YORK · SHARJAH

Copyright © Laurie Le Roux 2023

The right of Laurie Le Roux to be identified as author of this work has been asserted by the author in accordance with sections 77 and 78 of the Copyright, Designs and Patents Act 1988.

All rights reserved. No part of this publication may be reproduced, stored in a retrieval system, or transmitted in any form or by any means, electronic, mechanical, photocopying, recording, or otherwise, without the prior permission of the publishers.

Any person who commits any unauthorised act in relation to this publication may be liable to criminal prosecution and civil claims for damages.

This is a work of fiction. Names, characters, businesses, places, events, locales, and incidents are either the products of the author's imagination or used in a fictitious manner. Any resemblance to actual persons, living or dead, or actual events is purely coincidental.

A CIP catalogue record for this title is available from the British Library.

ISBN 9781035812912 (Paperback)
ISBN 9781035812929 (ePub e-book)

www.austinmacauley.com

First Published 2023
Austin Macauley Publishers Ltd®
1 Canada Square
Canary Wharf
London
E14 5AA

Many thanks to all those who supported me in the writing process, and who stood by my side in the realisation of the project; and many grateful thanks to Austin Macauley Publishers for making my dream come true.

Prologue

"STOP!" screamed Kyra. The gun pointed at her heart. The pain froze the blood in her veins, outstretched her tensed body. She was completely frozen, frightened. Her eyes were wide open. Her heart was furiously beating. What should she do? Solutions had blown out of her mind, she was lost, just lost and stray. She was gone, gone at the other end of the world. Gone somewhere she belonged. Her difference was her woe, the burden pulling her at the end of an isolated well. Her lungs were crushed by an overwhelming number of dilemmas. They were destroyed, hindering her of breathing. The cold air couldn't spread in her frozen body. She couldn't breathe anymore. She was stuck, struggling, the rope tightening around the soft skin of her neck. Her weight was calling her to her last breath. Would she support more of this pressure and tenseness? She hoped so. But she knew she would never do it. She knew it was her end.

"What do you mean?" asked the masked man in front of her. He examined her face, as if he could read inside her. His voice was warm and calming, like if none of the sorrow living in this room had ever reached him.

"I said, stop," she calmly repeated. Her heart pounded hard, her eyes blurred at his masked face, but she spoke quietly and confidently. She suddenly fell on her knees, a terrible ache piercing through her body. She breathed frantically, squinting at the black floor beneath her.

"They are taking revenge," she whispered painfully. "They alerted me already."

"And you ignored them?" asked the masked man, raising an eyebrow.

"It doesn't matter anyway. It would have happened, sooner or later."

Kyra put a hand down, the last of her force drifting away. The pain numbed her; her heart burned inside her. She could barely blink at the masked man in front of her, trembling uncontrollably.

"Help me, please," she begged, slobber running down her frozen lips. Her eyes looked blankly at an invisible point in front of her. Her left hand cowered on her heart, she breathed painfully.

"Help me," she uttered, with barely a stammer.

A sudden detonation overran the little room and a hoarse voice resounded in the silence,

"You're showering the symptoms of a cardiac disease," said a man, coming in as if he had been invited. His footsteps resounded in the empty whiteness of the room. He was like a black stain in this white place, a drop of black paint in a flowery field. The crow among the nightingales, the drums among the flutes. A freezing breeze in an empty room.

"LEAVE!" screamed Kyra, trying to stand up again.

The man laughed nastily, contemptuously looking at her.

"You can't avoid your fate, Kyra," he whispered into her ears. "We've decided what will happen to you. And your feebleness will never come back to contradict our plans."

"Leave her alone!" intervened the masked man. "She has the right to decide by herself."

"She can choose between two options," hummed the man in black. "Either she kills herself and avoid a long and painful death or wait and die in a painful way."

A long silence followed the man's words. Kyra stared at him for a long moment, before cringing reluctantly:

"I've never been weak."

The words broke in the frozen air, the temperature dropped abruptly, and a deadly silence spread across the room.

"What did you just say?" wheezed the man.

"I was just different from you, 'cause I could *feel* what you couldn't, I could be someone with a normal life, something that none of you ever manage to do! I wasn't a robotized number who blankly believed in your orders, I took revenge, I changed our lives! And you hate me for that, because the lovely and sweet routine you had suddenly faded away under your eyes!"

"I hate you because you're different! You should never have been like a fragile, weak, and feeble human being! You should have been more! Much more! And without feelings, heartless!"

The man plunged his hand in his pocket, caught his gun and pulled it out, his anger drowning the few feelings left into a hurricane of wrath. He lifted the tiny black arm, vising quickly, his shaking fingers on the trigger.

"I'll let you decide," he said in the most controlled way he could. "I will count until ten."

The masked man stayed next to him, frozen. Kyra fell miserably to the ground, her heart pounding hard. The electric twinge driving from her heart to her limbs caused her to lay on the marble, her voice snatched out. There was no noise to be said anymore, no words to save herself from the excruciating fate waiting on her path. Waiting so close. Waiting because she violated the law. The first and most important law in her world. The cause of her violation would tear her up until she surrendered.

She knew, she knew when she heard her heartbeats in the gap of the room, that what she expected would never happen. She had this talent, this kind of star shining in her eyes, showing that she would stand tall until the end. And that the end would be always surprising and different. And as far as she knew this very minute, she had still some time in front of her to face the truth and gather all the most important parts of her life. Because she was like a broken puzzle and the pieces were missing in her heart.

And she needed to gather them all. Just to feel as if she held a warming candle.

She closed her eyes, stopped listening to the man's cringing voice, still shaking dangerously from her sore heart.

"I will never surrender," she whispered to herself.

In her mind, she could see her father's face, gently smiling at her. Her mom, kissing her forehead before turning the light off. Her sisters, playing and sharing with her. Her classmates, fearing her from primary to high school. And all the passers-by she had always seen without knowing them. Her family's white house in Halifax. Their little apartment in Iceland. The landscapes she knew by heart, the colour that always appeared on the horizon. The way people used to talk, to move around, so different from one another. She could see their eyes looking at her, their mouths slowly articulating words she couldn't hear. Their faces. The sound. The hubbub around her.

She'd seen so many things. Too many things that marked her mind forever.

"I will never become HEARTLESS!" shouted powerfully the voice in her head.

***

Chapter 1
Alaska, USA

Elias Einarsson, 11 am, July 26th, 2018

"Why do you leave me?" asked a young girl, the tears running down her cheeks. "Why do you leave me?"

"I can't come with you, Kyra," whispered her mother, hugging her against her heart.

"Mama?" cried Kyra.

"You have to know that I love you, Kyra. I love you more than anything else. More than infinity."

"Don't leave me…" the young girl said, shivering. "It's cold outside, I need your arms to keep me warm."

"Kyra, live your life as you wish. If you feel alone, look into the shiny stars, you will see my smile from where you are."

"Mama…" whispered the young girl, trying to hide her tears. "How will I live without you?"

"I give you my life, honey. Being here is your way to success, to the fate waiting for you. And never look down, you're perfect as you are, Kyra."

"Don't leave me!" the young girl shivered again, frozen. "Don't leave me!"

"I can't stay. I love you, Kyra, I love you."

"Mama!" the young girl cried again, her voice struggling with the tears. "Mama!"

"I love you, Kyra."

The woman disappeared, leaving the child alone on her own.

"Mama!" called the young girl again, her voice fading away. But only silence responded. She quietly sat down, her tears falling on the ice at her feet. She tried to sing a song in her head to forget about the wildness of the place where she was left alone. But all the songs reminded her of her lost mother. Her mother who used to sing her these songs. She cowed her hands against her heart, trying to find a bit of warmth in the cruel cold surrounding her. She shivered again, her lips turning blue. She crossed her legs on the ice, looking around her through her tears. Maybe, her mother would come back and hug her, cuddle her, and tell her 'I'm sorry, sweetie, I forgot to tell you I would come back in ten minutes.' But no one appeared on the white horizon line. She was surrounded by whiteness and coldness, and she was lost, lost somewhere she didn't know.

"Mama, come back," she said, hoping.

She remembered what her mother told her and looked into the sky. But she couldn't see any stars. It was just white, like a blank lid upon her head. It was daytime. And it was cold. And she was lost, without parents. And she couldn't see any house. She dried her cheeks and stood up. She looked around her again and started walking. She didn't know where she was going. She didn't know if she would survive. But she was too young to know anything like this and the only thing she hoped was to find her mother, there, somewhere around her.

***

"Aliens exist," I said to my wife. "I know it."

"Well, have you been in touch with them? Do you know about their plans for the future? Do you think they will invade us and live on Earth, or they will stay in the galaxy?"

"Mandy," I tried.

"Elias," Mandy cut in. "Instead of dreaming about unbelievable things, why don't you go and check if Beverly's okay? She was playing in her bedroom last time I saw her, and I would like her to go play outside. And I will also need milk for tomorrow morning, and we are running out of bread, and meat and cereals. In other words, we have nothing to eat."

"Yeah, I will go shopping tomorrow, Mandy…"

"Elias, you've been saying that for five days and I can tell you that I am really running out of food," cut in Mandy again.

"Fine, I'm going to the grocery with Beverly, so she will go outside, and I will do the shopping."

"Wonderful," said Mandy.

I shook my head, not knowing what to say. I finally decided to fetch Beverly and came back with my daughter, holding her in my arms.

"Don't forget her tuque!" Mandy shouted from the kitchen.

"Have it!" I screamed back.

I sat Beverly on the chair and put her warm clothes on so she could go outside. In Barrow, in the northern part of Alaska, climate varied from -1° to 5° in July. Of course, some parts of Alaska were warmer than people could think of, but we didn't have the pleasure to live in such an area. We didn't really live in Alaska: Mandy, Beverly, and me. We were just here for a temporary displacement. And Beverly seemed to enjoy it. She was eighteen months old, and I could tell that she was the person who made me feel the happiest in the world. Her little smile when she grinned at me, her laughter, when she crawled or walked. Everything was so sweet and heart-warming.

"Elias!" shouted Mandy.

I turned and saw her looking at me, frowning.

"Didn't you forget something?" she asked.

I quickly checked everything. Beverly, dressed up in her warmest clothes, the car keys, my wallet, the bags… I had everything.

"No, I don't."

I saw Mandy smiling in front of me.

"And Beverly's tuque?"

The tuque. Where had I put it? I looked around me and noticed it in Mandy's hands.

"Be careful, Elias," she whispered, smiling.

I kissed her quickly and grabbed the tuque.

"Thanks."

I put it on Beverly's head and left the house, closing the door behind me. Beverly in my arms, I walked to the car and carefully opened the Jeep door.

"Papa," prattled Beverly.

"Yes, darling," I answered.

I looked at her. She was looking at a point in front of her, her fingers in her mouth like babies do.

"We're going to the grocery," I said.

"Papa!" she repeated.

I looked again at the black point in front of me.

"What?" I asked. "Have you seen Captain?"

Captain was our cat. She was tricolored and lovely, even though she was almost never there. I briefly looked, sure that Beverly had just seen Captain slowly moving around. But when Beverly started crying when I sat her down on her baby chair, I decided to look carefully. And what I saw was to give me goose bumps. A very little person was walking towards me, dangerously trembling, and shaking. The person wore no warm clothes. Only a thin jacket covered their skinny body. Their brown hair was falling over their eyes and I couldn't tell how old the person was until they looked at me.

"Is mama here?" she asked, looking at me.

I couldn't answer, my voice suddenly snatched out of my body. The little girl was around four years old. She had violet bags under her eyes and seemed about to fall on the ground, powerless.

"There is mama?" she insisted.

I knew Beverly was as silent as me, quietly looking at the poor little girl. She was lost, abandoned on her own in Alaska's immensity. And I couldn't find anything to say. I knew I should do something, but my brain was frozen and didn't want to react. I slowly took off my coat and put it on the girl's shoulders.

"Where is my mama?" she repeated, the tears falling down her cheeks.

"There is Mandy at home," I said carefully, not knowing what to do.

"Mandy not mama," she cried.

"But she can help you," I tried. "What's your name?" I asked.

"Kyra," she said.

"Come, Kyra, we will give you something at home. Let me pick up Beverly first."

I took Beverly in my arms again, closed the Jeep door and took Kyra's left hand, telling her to come with me. She followed me into the house, and I made her sit on the sofa. Mandy came in, frowning, about to ask me why I wasn't at the grocery shop but stopped when she saw Kyra. She briefly looked at me and went back into the kitchen, saying,

"I'll bring you hot chocolate."

I gave Kyra a hot blanket and told her I would be back in a few minutes. She nodded and I went to the kitchen too, still holding Beverly tightly.

"Who is it?" Mandy asked me as soon as I entered the kitchen.

"I don't know," I whispered. "She was there when I went in the garage with Beverly. She told me her name was Kyra and she's trying to find her mother."

"Her mom?" repeated Mandy. "Where's her mom?"

"I don't know," I answered. "Beverly saw her, I thought it was just Captain coming to ask for food."

"What should we do?"

"She will sleep here tonight, and then we'll go to the police, they'll know what to do."

I hugged Mandy as she took the pan out of the fire and poured the milk into a bowl. She added chocolate powder in it and gave it to me.

"She seems to like you," she simply said.

I put Beverly on the floor and took the hot bowl as I brought it to Kyra. I entered the living room few seconds later and found the girl still sitting on the couch.

"Here's your hot chocolate," I said.

She took it, analysing my face with her big brown eyes.

"Something's wrong?" I asked.

"Why do you want me to see police?" she asked with her sweet voice.

I stopped. See the police? Did she hear us? It didn't seem like she had moved from the sofa! She was still wearing my coat and sitting under the blanket. And the blanket was still in place, the way I placed it around her shoulders before leaving the room.

"I just heard you talking," she said, looking at her hot chocolate.

"No worries, Kyra," I responded.

The little girl was definitely intriguing.

"You should go and pick up Beverly," she whispered. Mandy will drop the burned pan soon."

I looked at her, not knowing if I should laugh, answer, keep looking at her, thank her, or go. I finally opted for the last option and walked back into the kitchen. Mandy was adjusting the pan on the fire and Beverly was silently crawling at her feet. I quietly walked to Beverly and picked her up before walking back to the living room.

"It's alright now," Kyra said, drinking her hot chocolate.

I sat down next to her, unable to say a word. Did she ask me to fetch Beverly to get my attention? Was she a fortune-teller? Mandy had never dropped any pan since I've met her. Why would it happen today? Did Kyra just say some random things to make me go away? I didn't know. And I didn't have to think more when a heard the pan crashing on the floor and Mandy protesting.

"No…" I heard Mandy saying from the kitchen.

"It's fine, Mandy," I heard myself say. "I will help you clean it."

Like a robot, I cuddled Beverly one more time and made her sit among her toys before walking to the kitchen, under Kyra's careful eyes.

***

Elias Einarsson, 6 pm, August 1st, 2018

"You have to explain me something, Kyra," I said.

I shook my head and took a big deep breath. How was I supposed to ask her if she was normal? It sounded weird. I closed my eyes, trying to figure out the best way to say it. *Mmh, I think there are weird things happening since you're there… are you normal yet?* Definitely not. That wasn't the way to say it. But Mandy and I had decided to adopt her, and Kyra would be a part of our family from now on. And I had to clarify some things if she was to live with us.

"It's hard to ask," I said. "But is there anything you have to tell me that might be very important?"

Kyra slowly shook her head.

"I don't think so," she responded.

"Is there anything you would like to tell me about your parents?"

"I never saw dad. Mom was nice, I miss her."

I put my hand on her shoulder. She was about to burst into tears.

"Alright, darling," I whispered. You can go and play now. We'll go back to Halifax tomorrow, and it will be a long journcy."

She shook her head and ran into her room, leaving me alone in the corridor. I longed to discover what she was hiding, because I knew she was, just couldn't figure anything out. There was no way, no way I could make her speak about her past or her. All I knew was that she was around four years old, her name was now Kyra Einarsson, and she was legally a part of our family. But I knew something was hidden.

Beverly seemed to like her and that was perfect at the moment. If Beverly agreed to be left in the same room as Kyra, I trusted these two little girls. I trusted them, even though I was quite uneasy about certain things, which I still couldn't explain.

Yesterday morning, Kyra walked into our room at 5 o'clock and whispered to my ear "*My mom said that one day, I will know why I was left on land.*" I didn't know what she meant by "left on land" and I didn't know what she meant at all, but I hoped one day, she would explain it to me. And I also hoped she would stop scaring me, walking and whispering in my ear in the middle of the night.

Furthermore, after the pan accident when I discovered Kyra, the strange little girl told me few things about what would happen soon after. She told me before we cooked the soup that my bowl would be way too salty. And it happened. It was freakish and no one else in the house knew about it. Kyra didn't talk much when Mandy was around and even though Mandy was a good mother, the two of them didn't seem to like each other. I still did my best to show both of my little girls that I loved them as much as one another.

"Elias!" called Mandy.

I jumped, falling to Earth again. What happened?

"Mandy?"

"I finished packing Beverly's stuff. Are you bringing the luggage to the garage?"

"No problem," I answered.

"And how is Kyra doing?" she asked.

"I don't know," I answered. "Well, I think. But I would like her to tell us what's wrong."

Mandy looked at me as if she was trying to understand what I meant.

"I mean, I think she's anxious about going to Halifax tomorrow. She's used to Alaska's landscape," I quickly rectified. "I will read her a book tonight with Beverly. I guess she will enjoy it."

"Yeah, she will."

Mandy looked at me once again and frowned before going back to our small office. I sighed and headed back to the bedroom where I had left some important papers. I walked pass Kyra's bedroom and entered, yawning. The different meetings I had today required a lot of energy and patience. We had stayed in the conference room for hours and hours, listening to endless speeches about new discoveries and machines that should change the world in the future. Our work was futurist and fascinating. We welcomed several important scientists and physicians today – and there was an intriguing discussion. They showed us pictures of what they had seen around Barrow a few days ago. The brightness of these pictures hid the tiny details, but everyone in the room – even those sitting at the back – could distinguish silhouettes. Tiny silhouettes that appeared on the horizon line like long black dots. And on this picture, I was sure, definitely sure, that I'd seen two persons. It wasn't something you could directly see, but it was there. My colleagues told me I was the only one to have seen such things, but when I talked to the scientist, he told me he'd seen them too.

In my opinion, life exists on other planets in our galaxy. But how could I prove it? My word wouldn't count much during an interview. All I needed to do, was to find a way to show it, using facts. Wouldn't be extraordinary if one day, I met one of them? I already had the whole set of questions I would ask them. I smiled and sat on the bed, still lost in my thoughts.

But I knew a lot about people's reactions. There was no place for extravagance and folly in this world. If something was to happen, it would have to be done quietly. It would have to be done hidden, to keep the secret and the magic living. Both important things, things that would make the world so different from what it is. And I knew. People were scared to face the truth. They knew what was going on but didn't want to learn more. They were fans of their silly routine. But I'd like the world to change somehow, to change into a different place where everybody would be respected and equal. But that was a dangerous path that only the bravest faced.

I sighed. It seemed so difficult to accomplish something important. I wanted to figure out something that no one ever did; I wanted to become an emblematic symbol that everyone knows. I lay on the bed, letting the darkness surround me. It was quiet. Quiet and calm. I could hear Mandy talking from the living room, and the unarticulated words Beverly tried to say. I was one of the happiest men in the universe. I closed my eyes for a second, sighing.

"Elias?" called Mandy.

I jumped and opened my eyes, seeing Mandy standing in front of me. Her brown eyes looked at me with tenderness and I couldn't stop feeling so joyful and appeased.

"Have you seen Kyra?" she asked.

My heart missed a heartbeat.

"Kyra?" I repeated, tensed. "Isn't she in her bedroom?"

"She isn't", answered Mandy, softly.

I jumped to my feet, ran out of the bedroom, shouting "I'll be back soon" over my shoulder. I ran downstairs, caught my coat, and quickly put my shoes on before opening the door.

"Kyra! I shouted. Kyra!"

I closed the door behind me, carefully listening. I shivered in the cold, squinting to have a better view. The sun was almost completely down, and the night was about to cover the sky. If I didn't find Kyra now, it would be impossible for her to find the way back home if she was walking away. And it would also be impossible for me to find her.

"Kyra!" I screamed again, my heart pounding.

A cold ran down my back and I frantically ran around the house. Where was she? Where did she go?

"KYRA!"

Panicking, I turned on myself a few times, looking around. But there was nothing. Not a single silhouette to be seen in the darkness of the coming night.

"Kyra!"

If she didn't come back, she would be lost. The temperature in Barrow was incredibly low, even in summer. I had to find her. But where was she? I shivered again. The vicious cold spread in my veins, freezing my lungs. I desperately ran towards the west. Few metres away from the house, I stopped again. What if she went the other direction?

What if I never found her again? I briefly shook my head, spinning to check if I could see her walking somewhere. I needed to calm down, to control myself. But where did she go?

"Kyra! Come back!"

A yellow light brightened the outside. I looked towards the house. Mandy was shivering on the steps.

"Kyra isn't in the house!" she said. "But she drew something on a piece of paper she found, look…"

I ran to the house and closed the door behind me. Mandy gave me the piece of paper and I briefly looked at it. There were some colours staining the white paper, some shapes one after another. But when I looked closely, I peeked an important detail on the corner of the page. A little scrawl that could look like an *e.*

"You found something?" asked Mandy.

"I'm not sure," I replied, "but I'll try. Stay here in case she comes back."

I jumped outside again and started running to the east.

***

"Mama…" called Kyra, sitting on the ground.

She had left the house without saying a word, escaping from them. She shouldn't have run away, she knew it, but she had to think for some time. Since she had arrived, she had learnt a lot, observing and detailing people's routines and twitches. The way they used to talk. The way they used to miss important information. She had seen how Elias and Mandy loved each other. And the way they were looking at each other destroyed her even more.

"Mama, why you don't come and grab me?" she said in her high voice. "I stayed and I saw them, now I want to see you smiling to me again".

She looked down at the ground beneath her, her breath quickening. When she was in Elias's home, she felt too much at the same time to know how to deal with her emotions. The tiny anger, the huge amount of love, of happiness, of airiness. She wasn't used to meeting open-minded people. They agreed to educate her, to keep her as a part of their own family. And it was probably one of the most startling things she had ever seen.

Kyra dried the tear which had fallen from her eye and cowed her hands against her heart, trying to find a bit of warmth inside her. She knew she was different from all other people on earth. She knew that one day, she would suffer because of what she was. And not because of what she would have done.

At this exact moment, she could feel the trouble coursing into her veins, the panic driving into Elias's body, the stress in Mandy's eyes. Her heart pounded hard for feelings she didn't own, and it drove her crazy. It was powerful and disconcerting. She didn't know how to appease her heart, her mind, how to calm her emotions, to stop feeling this confusion. Kyra shivered again in the cold of the wildness. If only someone could come, and explain her what was happening, it would release her from a burden. If she stayed there, sitting in the middle of nowhere, she might find a solution to her dilemma. But she might also stay here and find nothing, despite Alaska's cold temperature.

"Kyra!"

She jumped on her feet, frantically looking around.

"Kyra!" the voice screamed again.

Elias. She peeked quickly to her left, distinguishing a blurred silhouette running on the horizon. Without knowing what she was doing, she lay on the ground and crawled away, trying to be as discreet as she could. Her ears on the ground, she could feel Elias's footsteps getting closer and closer as she silently escaped. He would catch her in few minutes, she knew it. Her heartbeats resounding in the quiet landscape, she crawled away, Elias running behind her.

"Kyra, stop!" screamed Elias.

She didn't answer, just stopped, and turned to face Elias. He stopped in front of her, panting.

"You should never do that," he briefly articulated, hands on his knees. "Kyra, I told you, you can tell me everything. If you need help, I'll be there, listening to you. But don't run away like that! Please, don't."

Kyra looked at the horizon line, not knowing what to do. Running away, or simply stay and try to hide all the emotions giving birth to a hurricane inside her? She closed her eyes for a moment. She breathed as calmly as she could, letting her blood spread into her veins. She focused on the silence surrounding her. The quietness was soothing, placating. The cold travelled to her lungs. The air she was breathing in was cold, frozen. It had this unique smell of Barrow. The unique smell of Alaska. And the breeze calmly caressed her skin like soft feathers. The electric sensations bursting into little stars in her heart made her feel good. A smile stretched her lips as she listened to the song playing in her head. A song of happiness. Tranquil and quiet.

Kyra slowly opened her eyes and turned to Elias. He was standing next to her, holding his phone. He had turned on his flashlight to brighten the landscape.

***

Elias Einarsson, 6 pm, August 1st, 2018

When Kyra turned to look at me, I looked into her eyes, worried, but the gleam in her eyes send a thrill of horror down my spine. What I had seen was the most unbelievable thing that could happen to me. I knew it was dark at this exact moment, but I knew what I saw, and I could swear it. Her eyes were black. Completely black. I couldn't distinguish the pupil from the iris, nor the sclera. Everything had turned black – it was as dark as ebony. But there was something more. They were shiny. They seemed flamboyant and glowing, the flashlight reflecting into her eyes.

I was frozen. I was just standing in front of her, lost. I didn't know what to do. I didn't know what to say. There was nothing to be said. I was just standing there, my mouth opened wide and my eyes looking into hers. It was disconcerting. It was frightening. My face was stuck in a wince. And the only clever thing I could think of saying was,

"Goodness, what's that?!" abruptly breaking the silence.

Kyra looked at me, uneasy.

"I know I am strange," she said, looking away. "I want not to annoy you".

"That's why you left?" I asked, sitting next to her.

She shook her head.

"Why? I will never let you down, Kyra. I just want to know what's happening."

The little girl looked at me as if I'd said the weirdest words ever, frowning. I simply smiled, before continuing,

"You know, all I want is to understand you to make sure I can educate you better, nothing else."

Kyra remained silent.

"Do you know what's going on?" I asked.

"No," answered Kyra. "Mom does."

"Your mom?" I asked. "Where's she?"

"She left me on Earth, not telling why. I miss her," she added.

I sighed, thinking carefully.

"Is there any way we can ask her the questions we ask ourselves?"

Kyra looked into the sky over our head, silent for a moment.

"She said she in sky. Smiling in stars."

I looked at the stars as well. They were beautiful, shining upon our heads in the dark sky. They were tiny glowing and sparkling dots on this infinite darkness surrounding us. They were beautiful, astounding even. They brightened our small silhouettes sitting on Alaska's untamed floor. They seemed to be like a mom's careful eyes, cautiously looking at us.

"It's smashing," Kyra whispered next to me.

"It is," I answered, murmuring. "You made me discover this, Kyra."

The little girl turned to see me, detailing my face with her black eyes. I turned to face her, silent. She seemed calm, as if she was a normal child simply sitting in her bedroom. I let her think carefully, her tiny hands lying on her knees. She was cute. Cute and lovely, even though she was particularly strange. But I liked it. She was different. The way she was herself was unique and peerless.

Suddenly, a shiny and flamboyant light exploded around us, brightening the night. I jumped and Kyra hugged me, her little head on my heart. She was shivering in my arms, so fragile and tiny in this whole world. I hugged her back, squinting to peek in the sudden brightness. My heart was beating hard, and I hoped Kyra wouldn't feel it. I tried to hide my anxiety, holding her tight in my arms. It seemed to help me. I breathed slowly and deeply, analysing the situation. It couldn't be that bad.

Another bang exploded around us, and a long silhouette appeared suddenly in the light. The person materialized in front of us, tall and thin, standing straight and royally. Things could get worse in the end. I swallowed with difficulty, trying to look brave and strong to this stranger. But I wasn't. Someone has just appeared in front of me while I was sitting next to an orphan in the middle of Alaska. That wasn't a classical thing seen in everyday routine. First of all, it was impossible to appear suddenly from nowhere. Secondly, it was impossible to brighten the night without using a projector or an extremely powerful flashlight. And thirdly, it was impossible for a human to be surrounded by light. For a *human*. Was I sitting in front of an extraordinary creature? Was I sitting in front of extra-terrestrial monsters? What if Kyra was a part of them? And what if her mother was coming back to Earth to pick her up and kill me? I needed to calm down. I definitely needed to calm down and stop overthinking.

The person standing in front of us slowly sat down. I could barely see their face because of the light surrounding them, and a sudden cold ran down my back. It was even colder than it was before. And it was also brighter.

"Thank you, dear sir," whispered a sweet voice.

It was as sweet as soft silk, smooth, and mild.

"Who are you?" I answered.

"Kyra's mother."

The light suddenly turned off. I blinked a few times before squinting at her. She was beautiful. Her long blonde hair fell on her shoulders like a waterfall. She looked at me with her shiny eyes, as if she could read me. She somehow hypnotized me, slowly blinking. Her long eyelashes beat the cold air around us. She seemed calm, like if all of this was perfectly normal.

"Kyra's mother…" I repeated.

The little girl hadn't spoken since the light had brightened the night and the coldness of Alaska. I was wondering if all of this wasn't only a twisted dream, but I understood it wasn't when Kyra stood up. She momentarily stopped hugging me and walked to her mother. She lifted her arm but stopped.

"Mama…" she simply said.

"Darling, I can't stay," she answered. "Mr Einarsson, I leave you my daughter. Please educate her as best as you can."

"But how?" I asked.

"Mr Einarsson, my daughter has been banished from our clan," she briefly explained. You have to keep her away from her opponents."

"Which opponents?"

"Mr Einarsson, you are the only one I trust on this Earth: you are open-minded, and you believe in things you can't prove."

"What do you mean?"

"I mean that you are right Mr Einarsson. There are things which are true, but people don't believe in. There are things which are true and that you can't prove. Life is not limited to earth's boundaries; there are other forms of life too, outside your world: but you can't tell anyone. Please, promise me you won't say anything to anyone. And Kyra's identity has to stay secret. When you'll be back in Halifax, find Mr Flores. He will help you. I have to go now; I am not allowed to come here."

She stood up under Kyra's sad eyes.

"I love you, Kyra."

The light brightened, one more time, Alaska's cold landscape and she disappeared in a surprising bang. I stayed still. Kyra stayed still. We needed time to absorb all this information.

You are right, Mr Einarsson, but you can't prove it.

It meant that certain things could exist, even though you couldn't scientifically prove them.

Chapter 2
Halifax, Nova Scotia, Canada

Kyra Einarsson, September 1st, 2031

"Don't show them, don't tell them," I whispered.

I tied my hair up into a ponytail and sighed. Elias had already told me. He had told me that everything would be harder than for anyone else. He had told me it would be hard to hide who I was. And I always believed so. I had already been confronted to the hardest since I was born and telling me, every single day, that I would never be like anyone else, became a routine. Elias had told me from Mr. Flores that there was no one on Earth like me. This news was like a dagger to me. It pressed harder and harder against my heart, every single day. I wished I could talk to someone who could understand me; someone who could understand me *because* they were like me. And not just show pettiness in their innocent eyes.

I walked to the door and put my shoes on, lost in my thoughts. I knew one day I would find someone like me. And I also knew that one day, I would suffer from it. But I hid what I knew because no one could change the future anyway.

"I am proud of you," Elias smiled at me. "You're a beautiful person, Kyra."

I jumped and turned to face him, surprised. Elias was standing in front of me, a red cap on his head. I grinned back, holding my black school bag from one hand.

"Everything will be alright," he told me.

"I know, dad."

I jumped into his open arms and hugged him tightly.

"Thanks," I murmured unwillingly.

"What for?" he laughed.

"For being here when I needed you," I answered, blushing.

Elias simply looked at me, smiling.

"It's time to go to school now," he said. "Go to the car, I will fetch Beverly and we leave."

"Dad," I said.

"Oh, I'm sorry, Kyra," he apologized.

"It's alright," I sighed. "I need to go now, bye!"

I picked up my skateboard and waved before leaving our house. I put my earphones on and unlocked my phone, slowly driving my skateboard on the road. Which song should I listen to? I sighed and chose one of my favourite songs. I needed to be strong for this new school year and I knew I would draw my forces from this song. The notes started playing and I briefly closed my eyes. The upcoming year would be one of the years I had been waiting for. I felt it.

I turned right at the next road and pushed harder. Rapidity was one of the things I loved in all activities. From riding a motorcycle to skiing, it was one of the most beautiful things I had ever felt. The adrenaline driving in my veins, a frozen smile on my face and my heartbeats quickening over and over again… The first sport I had been taught was skiing. And this envy to go faster as I slid down the hill grew in all other sports.

When I was five, I discovered martial arts. And since then, I changed immensely. I didn't know how, but I did. During an international martial art show, I discovered the capoeira. The capoeira, or the dance of war. This martial art combined dance, acrobatics, and music. It was first introduced in Brazil around the 1600s. And a few years later, when I reached seven or eight years old, Mr Flores introduced me to Ninjutsu. This Japanese martial art was taught to Japanese spies, most commonly known as ninjas. Since I discovered these two pearls, I attended all my classes at the academy. It was a need as well as a hobby.

I grinned, reminding myself of these two moments. One day, I may like to start something new. There were so many different martial arts that seem so interesting and special.

"Hey, Kyra!" shouted someone.

I barely heard Callie behind me and took my earphones off, suddenly coming back to Earth.

"You passed by me without even noticing!" she yelled.

"Good morning, Callie," I laughed and opened my arms to hug her.

"Are you kidding me?" she said, falsely offended. "You want me to hug you, while you've just ignored me? Nah…"

She laughed and asked, walking beside me,

"So, how was your summer?"

"We went to Iceland to see my father's family," I responded with a neutral voice.

"How was it?" asked Callie, her eyes shining with stars.

"I brought you souvenirs," I smiled. "You'll come after school tonight and I'll give them to you."

"Oh, Kyra thanks!" she hugged me.

"No problem."

We walked to the school and slowly entered the building, stuck in the crowd. The hallway and corridors were full of young people walking and chatting by the lockers, looking without noticing at the people opening and closing their lockers.

"Another year's waiting for us," sighed Callie. "It's going to be even harder than before."

"Probably," I answered. "Do you know where we have to go?"

"No, we'll see!"

Callie and I walked around the school, rediscovering the old corridors. The old smell still floated in the air like it did every single day. The stuffy atmosphere rapidly evaporated when Callie opened the window and sat on the windowsill, smiling. She looked at me as if she was carefully thinking. I simply watched her, not knowing what to do. When I saw she wouldn't say anything, I turned to face the entrance. More and more students were entering, listening to music, or checking their phones. They wore their simplest clothes, jeans and sweatshirt, or their best clothes for the first day. I yawned and turned to face the window when my eyes stopped on something. Or someone.

I looked twice, briefly peeking at the mob. A boy with blue hair had just entered the school, holding his skateboard with one hand and his phone in the other. One of his earphones was hanging on his black sweatshirt while the other one was playing in his ears. His lips were stretched into an impish smile. His left leg was gently tapping the floor to the silent notes only he could hear. He briefly seeked someone in the mob and stopped on me, grinning. I smiled back and he softly pushed the students around him to reach me.

"Kyra," he said when he stopped by me. "Here you are."

"Nathaniel," I smiled. "Always arriving at the very last moment."

The bell rang loudly in the school and the hurrying students started rushing in the corridors. People ran along them, looking for their classes.

"Are you kidding me?" he laughed. "How are you, Callie?"

"Fine thanks," she answered jumping from the edge of the window.

"Hey, Nathaniel!" shouted a young man arriving behind him. "We're going to the skate park tonight. You joining? There will be a competition against the Teigr's clan at ten o'clock tonight. Be there."

"Sure, Loven," answered Nathaniel, shaking his head. "It's always important to show the Teigr who's the best."

"You're also invited, Kyra," added the young man. "The more we are, the greater are our chances to win."

"I'll be there," I smiled. "The Kitsune will always win as long as Xi' will be governing it."

"Don't forget to dress up," answered Loven. "It's going to be important tonight. The first ceremony of the year has to be celebrated. There will be an opening with skateboarders and then we'll start the competition."

***

The Kitsune were hiding behind one of the buildings in Halifax. The twenty-one skateboarders were silent, looking carefully at the passers-by innocently walking in the empty streets. The temperature was low and the fresh air blowing between the buildings brought adrenaline and stress. The mix of emotions and the smell of hot chocolate spreading from one of the open windows brought strangeness to the evening. What was about to happen was unique and the Kitsune enjoyed every single breath filled with adrenaline. In the silent and cold night, one of the masked silhouettes quietly tiptoed to another silhouette standing in front of the others, holding a skateboard under his arm.

"Are we going to the warehouses?"

"We are," whispered Xi'. "Go back to your place."

Quietly holding their skateboards, the twenty-one members of the Kitsune clan tiptoed from one building to another, slowly getting to the warehouses. It was past nine o'clock and the cold breeze of the night already whispered in the empty streets. No noise was to be heard and not even the Kitsune clan troubled the still and smooth silence.

"The Teigr will be there already," whispered someone to my ear.

I jumped and turned to face the masked clan's member.

"We will never be late," I murmured back.

I looked into the member's dark eyes. They were neutral, not letting any emotions stain their stars shining under the moon's white light. I simply smiled and turned back, running behind the others, holding my skateboard in my right hand. The members of the Kitsune clan were dressed up in black from head to toe, hiding their identity underneath clothes. Only their eyes could be seen, and their name known.

"Get on," whispered someone, turning to face us.

We silently put our skateboard on the ground and quietly pushed down on the road. The slipping silhouettes drove easily in Halifax's streets, running to the abandoned warehouses in the countryside. I felt the cold surrounding us. The temperature outside was cool and as I drove pass many streets, the breeze quietly caressed my cheeks. I calmly breathed and quickened to reach Loven and Nathaniel, a few metres away. Nathaniel briefly turned to face me, a smile stretching his lips.

"Stressed?"

"Not yet," I answered. "It takes place every year, it's like a simple family dinner on a Sunday afternoon."

"A family dinner?" silently laughed Nathaniel. "You have a lot of imagination. But it's still a competition," he added nervously. "You should be prepared to win for the Kitsune clan."

"I know that if I fail, you will be there to save us all," I replied.

"Hush!" cut Loven. "We're there."

I adjusted my hood so that only my eyes could be seen and put on my black gloves. We silently entered the derelict warehouses and stopped by the parking. Xi' put down his skateboard and so did we, the adrenaline already driving in our veins.

In front of us were standing twenty-one other silhouettes dressed up in dark grey, holding their skateboards with a nonchalant gesture. Behind them were the ropes on which we would be soon competing. The Teigr's leader and Xi' walked to each other and briefly shook hands.

"The first competition is about to start," suddenly said the Teigr's leader, his voice bursting the night's silence.

Whispers ran through the two clans facing each other. *It was about to start.* I shivered, the adrenaline rapidly growing inside me.

"This year will be an important year for the two clans," shouted Xi', so we could hear him.

"They will celebrate their fifteenth anniversary. The three best players of each clan will fight for their clan. The best clan will then be determined."

Nathaniel briefly turned to face me. They had changed the game and it would be harder than before. Stress drove into my veins, and I winced.

"Calm down," suggested Loven, barely looking into my eyes. "Tell yourself it's like an exercise."

I took a deep breath, desperately trying to slow down my heartbeats. Fading to panic now would be a bad idea. Stressed, my heart pounding hard, I tried to focus on Xi's speech, but my ears buzzed dangerously, and I could barely hear him. I yawned, trying to figure out how I could be standing without using all my energy. I felt so powerless… Like if I was going to fall and not be able to stand up again… I felt dizzy and coughed a few times trying to keep my balance. Was the Earth moving so fast? I couldn't stand anymore. My knees wouldn't support my weight no longer and I would be falling…

"Kyra!" someone screamed.

Little colourful stars appeared in front of my eyes and blurred my vision. My ears buzzed louder and louder, and I soon couldn't hear anyone talking. The temperature around me jumped higher and higher and I felt as if I was falling into a well. My eyes suddenly opened wide, and I glanced at Loven as if I had just met him for the first time.

"Are you okay?" he asked me, worried.

The whole Kitsune clan was standing around me.

"What's happening?" I articulated with difficultly.

I could barely breathe, lying on the cold parking. The silence around us was awkward and unpleasant, like if something was about to happen.

"I feel like I can't stand anymore…" I said between two coughs.

"Have you eaten lately?" asked Loven, uneasy.

"Yeah, this supper, why?" I asked, coughing again. "I feel like I can't breathe."

"Does it often happen to you?" questioned someone else standing behind Xi'.

"It already happened… but not that bad."

"How often does it happen?" insisted the same masked person.

"Regularly," I coughed again.

My chest dangerously ached, and I sat down, cowering my arms against my heart.

"Kyra," whispered Loven. "If you want, I can take you to the hospital."

I slowly shook my head.

"The competition just started; I can't leave like that."

"Don't be silly," gently scold Nathaniel. "You can't even stand up anymore."

I looked down, knowing they were right.

"Fine. In that case, I need to see Elias. He will know what to do. But one of you has to stay and win the competition for me. Please," I added.

Loven helped me get on my legs and we both silently left after Nathaniel told Xi' everything would be alright. We silently walked out of the warehouses, lost in our thoughts. From where we were, we couldn't hear the Kitsune nor the Teigr and had no clue about the competition's progress. I held my skateboard under my right arm, caressing its surface with my fingertips. My heart pinched when I suddenly heard claims coming from the warehouse parking lot. Was it for the Teigr or for us, the Kitsune? I had no idea. I sighed and stumbled on the road, Loven next to me.

"Don't worry, it will be okay," he said with a tight throat. "The Kitsune will win for us".

I nodded to show I heard and continued walking, Loven supporting me.

"Sit down. I will call your father," he said. "You won't be able to go back home like this."

I shook my head and sat on my skateboard, unlocking my phone and giving it to Loven. He touched the screen a few times and listened silently to the ringing bell. I yawned and put my head in my arms, closing my eyes. I wanted to be home already, listening to music under a warm blanket instead of freezing in the abandoned countryside. I shivered as the cold breeze whispered in the dark street. The darkness surrounding us seemed to be frozen, like if it was holding their breath to not break the silence. The freezing coldness floated around our silhouettes, cooling our body temperatures. There was no flavour in this frozen air, no emotions travelling around, just a long silence. And we were in the middle, waiting for Elias to answer the phone.

"Mr Einarsson," suddenly said Loven. "Can you pick us up? We are at the warehouses and Kyra is unable to walk."

"What happened?" I heard Elias asked, uneasy.

"We don't really know…" answered Loven hesitantly.

"Don't stir from where you are, I will be there in few minutes."

"Alright, thank you, Mr Einarsson."

Loven ended the phone call and turned off my phone before giving it back to me. He briefly smiled and turned, looking further away in the street. I remained silent, looking at the asphalt beneath my feet. I checked the time on my phone and turned it off again, nervous. The silence in the street was awkward and if nothing happened in the next seconds, I would start panicking again.

"Thank you for staying with me," I said, breaking the silence. "You're missing the competition for that."

"The competition isn't a problem," answered Loven. "The others will compete for us."

I looked at him curious.

"You know, what you've just lived..." he continued. "It always happens to me. I've been to the doctor a few times already. But there's nothing we can do about it. I mean, there's nothing he can do for me. He might be able to save you."

"What is it?" I asked.

Loven turned to face me, looking into my eyes. A bright star shone in his blue eyes. It was the first time I noticed it. In his dark blue eyes, stars were shining like in a summer night sky. Calm but flamboyant. Respect and truth gleamed in his eyes. It was warming. Comforting, even.

"Something that will never forbid me from living," he murmured.

His skateboard slipped on the road and stopped in front of me. Loven smiled and opened his arms, detailing my expression. The coldness of the night suddenly disappeared and all I could feel were these little butterflies flying around in my stomach. Warmth spread in my veins, driving from my heart to my fingertips and my frozen nose. Heat drove in my cheeks, and I blushed, burying my head in his neck. I huddled in his warm arms, closing my eyes and breathing in the magic chemicals moving between us. The street seemed to be breathing again; the unpleasant silence evaporated; the surrounding darkness fled from us. The derelict place seemed to live again.

I hugged him tightly, forgetting about the real life around us. Suddenly, my heartache stopped, my pain and my aches ended, and I could breathe normally. This unique moment, these peerless seconds flew like sand in the hourglass. They were like diamonds to me, special and particular, sparkling with different emotions.

"My heart is my life," murmured Loven. "As long as it beats, I will be living like no one else ever did. The competition is just a short paragraph in the story of my life. If I preferred spending this time with you instead, it's because you are much more."

He stopped and I listened carefully, my heart pounding hard. The butterflies still flew in my stomach, but my stress increased rapidly. I couldn't feel anything; it was as if I was flying on warming clouds. I couldn't see anything despite his black sweatshirt. I could only hear his voice softly speaking in the night.

"Every time I look at you, I see in your eyes things I've never seen before. Your eyes are the ones that speak without talking. You're different and unique, and I feel like I would never be able to look away from you."

He gently pulled me towards him, so I faced him. His eyes read through me as if I were a book. This disconcerting manner of smiling made my heartbeats quicken. My arms were trembling, and I was shivering, his hands on my shoulders. The cold hit me again and all the warming atmosphere we built up disappeared in a second, leaving behind another dark and isolated street. But the noise invading the cold place was thunderous. My heartbeats mixed with the seconds, the streetlamp's sizzle and the shouts from the warehouses. *He...* I saw him stretching his lips, forming words, and like a film where the sound is delayed compared to the image, I heard him pronouncing these three meaningful words...

"I love you."

My heart briefly stopped beating and my face froze into an indecipherable poker face.

"Loven..." I murmured, tensed.

All the beauty and uniqueness of the streets disappeared to leave two friends talking.

"But you don't," he coldly replied, tensed.

"I..." I tried.

"You don't have to say anything," bitterly cut in Loven.

My heart pinched one more time.

"Then... if it is your wish... I will say no more," I said, turning to face the street.

Inside me, the butterflies were gone, and I could only feel my heart being torn apart and falling like broken glass on a snowy ground. I pinched my lips together and looked once again at the tar underneath my feet. It was as black and distant as Loven. Like the warehouses, the bitumen was forlorn. And like Loven, it was forsaken. I felt Loven's pain driving in his veins, darkening his heart, and soiling his mind. My words must have hurt like poison to his senses and feelings, and I was sitting next to him, a watcher of all his woe.

"I'm sorry," I murmured for myself.

"You don't have to," sharply said Loven. "You're freeing me."

I turned around and looked at him.

"What do you mean?"

Elias's car suddenly appeared on the road. His highlight bursting into the obscurity. I jumped, looking again into Loven's eyes.

"What do you mean?" I insisted.

He didn't answer me, and the car stopped by us. A door slammed and Elias appeared behind him, distraught.

"Kyra!" he called when he saw me. "Are you okay? We have to go to the hospital, do we?"

He quickly opened the car's door and helped me sit on the backseats under Loven's careful eyes.

"Come in, Loven, we'll bring you back to your home."

"It's not necessary, Mr Einarsson, thank you for the invitation," he coldly replied.

He stood up and jumped on his skateboard before fading in the streets. Elias and I looked at the point where he vanished, frozen.

"We're going back home," announced Elias, giving me my skateboard, and slamming the door again. He entered the car and sat down, turning on the car. He briefly looked at me in the mirror, uneasy. He opened his mouth as if to talk, hesitated and closed it. He didn't ask any questions and we drove through the night, heading back to Halifax.

***

Kyra Einarsson, September 4th, 2031

I was waiting for a long time in hospital, glancing at the white floor underneath my feet, my hands in my pocket and my grey hoodie on. My breathing was spaced and calm. There was no noise in the waiting room, despite the buzz of the lightbulbs and the ticking of an old man's watch. He was sitting in front of me, as frozen as I was, fixing the white floor, lost in his thoughts.

Elias had stayed with me for a long time, but he had an important conference that day and had left me all alone in one of the hospital's waiting rooms. I sighed silently, looking at the revues on the small table in the middle of the room. Celebrities were posing on the colourful cover, wearing bright and flashy clothes. On one of them was posing my mom.

Mandy was standing on the cover of her new album, holding a key in her left hand and a lock in her right hand. She had recently left for her six-month tour in Europe. I sighed, thinking about Beverly and Rachel, my two younger sisters. When I first saw Beverly, she was around one year and a half. She would celebrate her fifteenth birthday next week in an amusement park with her friends. And I would stay home with Rachel, while Mandy would be singing in Italy and Elias discussing in a scientist's conference in Manitoba.

I sighed again. All I was trying to do was to avoid thinking about my results. I hoped nothing was wrong. I hoped everything would be alright. But I could feel inside me that my hopes would never come true.

"Ms Einarsson?" asked someone.

I jumped up. One of the nurses was standing by the door, the doctor standing behind her. As I noticed them, my heartbeats quickened, and my head started spinning. My hands were moist, my vision was glued to them. *What were the results showing*? I could feel their emotions at this very moment. And before they told me, I knew.

***

Kyra Einarsson, September 6th, 2031

"So, what did the doctor say?" asked Nathaniel.

We were sitting in a cafe in the city centre, talking about the last events. Callie and Nathaniel were sitting in front of me, on the cafe's bench, holding their cup of coffee in one hand. Nathaniel wore a black bonnet covering his blue hair. Callie had tied up her hair in a ponytail and looked at me, curious. Both were listening to me as if they were drinking my words.

Since the last skateboarders' competition, I hadn't talked to Loven and neither had he. We tried to avoid each other in the school's corridors, always turning our backs or changing direction before getting too close. This habit destroyed me from the inside, but I didn't try anything to change it. I had to wait for the right time to do it. And I hoped it would be soon.

"The doctor said the symptoms were close to those hiding a heart fail," I answered. "But not all of them are present, which contradicts with the others. He said he didn't know what it was."

"But there must be something that can help you!" said Nathaniel.

"I'm going to hospital tomorrow," I said. "Maybe he will figure out something."

Silence followed my words. Nathaniel and Callie looked at me as if they were trying to find the best friend they used to know. I sighed, looking outside the window.

"He told me he knew quite a few people like me, but still nothing has been figured out," I added.

I looked outside, taking a sip of my coffee. I could feel my friends carefully analysing my face, as if I was going to fall on the bench, inanimate. I silently sighed, looking at the passers-by walking in the streets. They looked so innocent and carefree. Nothing was threatening them. Nothing was waiting, lurking a few paces away from them, menacing their lives. They had all the time they wanted to do what they were dreaming about. *Will never forbid me from living...* Loven's words resounded in my head. He was right. Nothing could come trouble us. We only had a few moments left in front of us. We should enjoy them.

My heart quickened when I caught somebody's eyes. Someone was standing in the middle of the passageway, glancing at the cafe. Or *in* the cafe. I looked into his dark blue eyes, shivering. Would he come in? Would he join us? Did he know? Did he know how much I missed him? We stayed frozen for few seconds, looking into each other's eyes. When I approached my hand from the glass, he turned and left, leaving me alone, my heart painfully pinching.

"Kyra?" asked Callie.

I suddenly fell back in the little cafe, my smile snatched away from my face.

"Loven was standing there," I said. "But he didn't come."

Nathaniel partially smiled, taking a sip of his coffee.

"What happened after you left the Kitsune competition?"

"We talked and Elias came to fetch me," I explained. Who won the competition?"

Nathaniel's smile disappeared and he cleared his voice.

"We lost," he said. "Xi' said that you were both supposed to be competing as the best players. But you both left. Nick was left and he asked the fourth and fifth best skateboarders to come with him, but we still lost."

I shook my head.

"I'm really sorry I left," I said. "But I would have been useless, I had no energy to stand up."

Nathaniel shrugged, looking away.

"We will win next time."

***

Chapter 3
Halifax, Nova Scotia, Canada

Kyra Einarsson, September 13th, 2031

My phone rang. I turned to check who sent the message and froze as I read the provenance. *Unknown number.* My heart missed a beat, and I opened it quickly, rapidly reading the message. *Halifax Airport, 3:20 pm.* I walked to my bed and kneeled. I stretched my arm under the bed and grabbed my emergency luggage, my heart pounding hard. I checked if I had my passport and grabbed my phone.

"*Callie,*" I texted. "*I have an important rendezvous this weekend and Elias isn't at home. Could you stay with Rachel and Beverly?*"

I sent the message and waited. I hoped she would answer soon… The clock had just turned to show 2:30 pm. I had fifty minutes to reach the airport.

"*Alright, they will have to come to my home, I also have to babysit my cousin,*" she answered.

"*Thanks, the keys are in the vase on the windowsill.*"

I wrote a quick letter for Callie and left it on the table. I ran back to Rachel's room and entered, rapidly telling her Callie would stay with her until I came back, probably during the night. My heart pounding hard, I left the house closing the door behind me, and called a taxi to arrive on time at the airport.

"Where're you going?" asked the taxi driver as he stopped by me.

"Halifax airport," I answered, panting.

I closed the door and we left, heading to the airport, driving in the huge empty highways. I could feel the emotions driving in people's veins at the airport. I could already see their faces in my head when I closed my eyes. Their dark hard luggage. The woman with her son and his bright teddy bear. In a few minutes, I would be standing by their side, pretending to be taking a plane.

I could already see the globe hanging from the roof, the little plane flying around it. All the windows and entry doors. The escalators leading to the departures to the United States. The area with the fast foods on the left and the shops on the right. I bought a sweatshirt in one of these shops one day. The hoodie was white. Halifax was written in capital letters, with underneath the longitude and latitude, and the province, Nova Scotia and finally Canada.

"We're here," said the taxi driver.

I quickly paid him and hurried to the airport, cautiously holding my luggage. I turned to see the hotel where I had already slept three or four times and entered the clean airport. The place was airy and bright. The floor was perfectly clean, and the grey globe still hung from the ceiling, the little plane slowly turning around it. The escalators leading to the departures to the United States where still in front of me. I took a deep breath, like if I had found the place I always wanted to be in and headed to the rectangular 'waiting place', with the fast-foods and shops.

On my way to one of the fast-foods, I noticed a man sitting on one of the benches. He was checking his phone, a luggage by his side. A tuque hid his hair, and he didn't move when I walked past him. I remained silent and stopped once in the queue to the fast-food. The woman in front of me carried a bright teddy bear and her son was happily singing at her feet, holding his dark luggage from one hand. I discreetly smiled and waited.

"*Excusez-moi*, sorry!" suddenly said someone.

I turned to face the man who was sitting on the bench a few seconds ago. He simply wanted to pass through the queue, certainly heading to the departures towards Europe. I moved backwards, carefully analysing his expression. He didn't add anything and disappeared, passing the security without a problem. My fingertips suddenly felt something in my pocket, and I pulled the paper out before opening it. "*Go to the observation room on the first floor.*" I sighed. It was almost my time to order. I left the queue and walked to the elevators.

I couldn't feel nor see the beauty of the place anymore. The smooth, mild atmosphere had gone to leave only an important mission. My face was now like a joker's. None of my emotions could be seen; none of my emotions reflected in winces or smiles. I detailed every single object I could see, from the chairs to the white lights indicating toilets or exits. I entered the small room and sat on one of the chairs, assessing every single person's face. Another man came to me a few seconds later and I tried to avoid the stress growing inside me.

"Here you are," the man said as if I was his daughter. "If you will, the plane is this way," he added. "Don't forget to change."

We walked for a couple of minutes, which appeared long to me. My heart pounded hard; my skin turned moist, my hands were shaking, and my lips were tightly pursed together.

"Emotions Itami," cringed the man by my side.

I took a big deep breath and tried to stay as calm as I could. I hadn't heard my code name for a while and I shivered, cold briefly running down my back. I would again face my fears to save the world, my face and identity hidden under a black cloth.

"Enter and change. In three minutes and twenty-nine seconds, you have to be at your seat, A12 for the departure. We will tell you about the instructions during the flight."

I nodded and entered the tiny bathroom, wrinkling my clothes out of my small luggage. I quickly dressed up and put my mask on before walking to my seat on the plane. Some spies were already seated, carefully working on their computers, or listening to music. I recognised some of them before sitting next to the porthole.

"Itami?" asked the spy sitting next to me.

"Tuga?"

We briefly shook hands before turning again, like if nothing ever happened.

The G.U.W.K. system was divided into three units working on different but related topics. The W.A.F., the spies were taught the basic and advanced technology of weapons. During their training, which lasted for four years, the world's armed fighters were told about the different uses and situations in which they evolved during their lives as intelligencers.

The second unit was the E.B.H.F., were fighters used to learn how to fight without weapons. The emergency bare hand fighters were intelligencers who were directly in contact with criminals. Their section was one of the most dangerous ones, with more killed and wounded than any other. I was a part of this limb of the G.U.W.K. System, secretly infiltrating houses, or businesses.

But these two units required the help of the V.T.S., whose whole unit was based on technology and computers. Their job was to discreetly infiltrate communication systems within a company and decode the daily text messages sent around the world. They kept the files and guided the E.B.H.F and the W.A.F., by virtual communication.

All of the intelligencers working for the G.U.W.K. system were highly protected by the association, and only the director of the agency knew their identity. All I knew from the others was their coded name. Their ages, their names, their profession, every bit of personal information was unknown to me. And it was the same for them. The point in the agency was to keep ignorance among the units, so nobody could report anything. The intelligencers were lonely and couldn't rely on anyone to save them.

"*Mission 337, Havana, Cuba.*" The electronic voice resounded in the plane, and I looked up at the white screen where the words slowly appeared in black ink. "*Mission 336 hasn't been completed by the former intelligencers. They were caught earlier in August. The compromising documents they had to take are now coveted by all other secret agencies running in the world. Their identity has been revealed and respects were offered to the victim's family. End the mission. So, their death wasn't in vain. Following instructions will be sent once arrived."*

The electronic voice died away and the bright screen turned off, leaving an unpleasant silence on board. I shivered again, turning to the window by my side. My heart dangerously pounded hard, and I winced, my hands shaking. It was harder than it was before, to save the world from a disaster. Death waited at all corners of the streets and avoiding it got harder and harder. Our enemies seemed to get stronger as they breathed; but we seemed to fade away.

The last unit sent was decimated. My heart pinched. This time, could it be us. Our enemies knew we would try to get the documents back. We wouldn't survive. I felt it. The trouble coursing into my veins grew bigger as the seconds passed. My breath quickened as my heart pounded even harder.

I thought about Beverly and Rachel, waiting at home. About Elias. He gave me the chance nobody would have given me. Should I try to escape? No. I couldn't. I had to face my future. I wouldn't run away like if I were scared. I would never show my real emotions.

Even though I was frantically looking through the window, I could feel the tension growing bigger as the minutes passed. And I knew that only one question floated in everyone's mind. *Would we survive?*

"Itami?" asked someone.

I turned to face Tuga, slightly shivering.

"You're stressed."

I briefly looked outside the window before answering:

"I can't hide my emotions anymore. I don't know what's going on."

Tuga shrugged.

"You should try to find a way to contain them, or we're all dying," he said scornfully.

I winced.

"When you say, 'hide your emotions', you'd better start from yourself and stop looking contemptuously at me."

He looked at me for several seconds.

"This is none of your business."

"It is, as we are in the same mission," I rapidly added "I don't want the whole intelligencers to die because you and I have been silly."

"Me, silly?" he repeated, almost smiling under his mask. "It's not my fault if my life's going like hell since the last few days."

"Watch your words!" shouted a voice.

We instantly stopped talking, listening. No one called us out again and we continued our talk, quietly whispering at each other's ears.

"Mine is also going like hell, but we have to forget about it," I murmured. "I remember the day I joined the system… They told me, live your life day by day, because you might never return from your missions. I accepted. I thought it would be easy. In fact, it's more like a routine than anything else. But living day by day is hard. I've planned a lot of things for the future; a future that I might never have."

Tuga had calmed down and softly whispered,

"We will achieve this mission. I will help you stay alive, for your future's plan, I promise. But mind your emotions".

"What about you?" I asked.

He sighed.

"It doesn't matter anyway."

"How?"

"You're too curious, Itami."

The plane landed at Havana, in Cuba, around eight and a half hours later. We stepped out of the plane and were given the instructions we had to follow. As soon as we entered the airport, we chose to follow different directions and within ten minutes, most of us were already gone. I was still standing in the middle of the shopping area, holding my luggage in one hand and a piece of paper in the other. The people around me were laughing and walking merrily towards the entrance or the exit, telling jokes or random anecdotes that I couldn't hear. I was standing in the middle of the hallway just as if I was frozen. I could feel the man's glance in my back and his hands ready to give heartless orders. I knew that if I didn't move in the next ten seconds, he would ask his men to grab me.

They were encircling me; I felt it. The sound of their paces against the floor resounded in the weakest vibrations, but I could still sense it. I could still sense it. Nine. His anger slowly appeared on his face, deforming his eyes into the dark eyes of a predator. I was the prey. I slowly turned my face in order to detail his face. Eight.

"This is the last mission I will do for you," I murmured underneath my breath.

Suddenly recovering, I grabbed my energy like if it was an object and left the airport, my heart pounding hard.

Once in the hotel where the G.U.W.K. had reserved a room, I grabbed my phone and sat on the bed, looking for

Callie's number. The plane had left at 3:30 pm and the arriving time was 11:00 pm, local hour. Callie, Beverly, and Rachel were probably already sleeping, as it was midnight in Halifax. I sighed and quickly sent her a message, asking if everything was alright. I quickly texted Elias and sent a message to Loven and Nathaniel.

Tomorrow would be the day when everything would be decided. And it would change something.

***

Kyra Einarsson, October 1st, 2031, 6 am

I woke up early in the morning and by the time the city was waking up, I was ready. I had cleaned everything in the room and my luggage was closed. Everything I needed was packed, and I was standing outside, detailing the smallest moves of the people around.

The water droplets fell slowly on the sidewalk as I watched the grey sky above me. The frigid breeze smoothly caressed my pinkish cheekbones, quietly whispering at my ears. I was surrounded by stiffness and anonymity. The beautiful city was for me nothing more than an isolated place where my fate was to be decided. My heart frantically pulsed as the time appeared long and stressful. In my head, the seconds repeated with the same unpleasant speed. I was expecting the worst to arrive in a black car. The decisive moment of my life would be sooner than I expected. I knew that the end wasn't far. The dark car peeped out on the road and silently stopped in front of me. Slightly shivering, I opened the door, sat and closed the door behind me as the car drove away.

"Are you ready, Itami?" questioned the man sitting next to me.

I nodded, hugging my luggage as if it could help me.

"I wish you the best," the man awkwardly said. "No failure will be accepted this time."

I nodded once again, not knowing what to say.

We drove to a place where I could stay with all the other intelligencers until the night. To enter the building, I had to change clothes again and adjust my hood so only my eyes could be seen. I left my luggage in a safe place and finally entered the building where a dozen other people were staying. Some were already working on computers, probably calculating the probability of chances the operation would work. Some were training in the far corner of the room, holding sticks and daggers. Others were training without weapons, breaking pieces of wood with their bare hands. They briefly looked at me when I entered, before continuing their previous occupations.

"You know what to do," the man said to me. "All information you need is on your instruction paper. The van will come at exactly eighteen hundred hours. You'll have to be ready by this time."

I once again nodded, showing that I had understood.

Chapter 4
Havana, Cuba

Dead Claw, October 1st, 11:59 pm

"Turn the light off," ordered Dead Claw in the walkie-talkie.

He silently stood in the middle of the room, looking through the glass of the window on the ninth floor. The night was already down, and darkness hid the details of the outside. The streetlamps stretched in the darkness like bright little dots. Smoke floated on the bitumen; the wind caused the trees to bend. A stormy night was waking up in the ignorance of the world. Dead Claw's rejoicing grew up inside him like dead poison and spilled in his vein, darkening his heart.

From the ninth floor of the building, he could barely perceive his men waiting outside. Their blurred silhouettes slowly moved around the dark trees, their hood carefully covering their faces. His men moved around like tiny ants in their anthill. A smile stretched his lips as he perceived a small van driving between the spotted lines of light in the road. He smiled, satisfied.

"They are coming," one of his men said in the walkie-talkie.

"Be ready," he answered.

He turned his walkie-talkie off and walked to a bucket he kept in the corner of the room. He carefully spilled the flammable liquid around the room. Before leaving the room, he looked for a lighter in his pockets and set fire to the room, carefully closing the door behind him.

"They are entering the building."

"Plan-A in action at the ground floor," ordered Dead Claw. "And don't forget," he added. "No survivors."

Dead Claw ran to the stairs and quickly ran to the ground floor. The first action of the plan was already executed and in less than eight minutes, the second group of intelligencers of the G.U.W.K. agency would be reduced to a ridiculously low number. Once he arrived at the ground floor, Dead Claw stopped in a dark corner, watching his men face the intelligencers. Around nine intelligencers had entered the building and his men were easily encircling them, blocking the doors and windows. The spies wore black clothes and a black hood; it was impossible to discern any facial features by looking at them. Only their height and structure varied from small and thin to tall and muscular. Around them stood his men, whose bulletproof vests shone in the moonlight.

Dead Claw watched his men and the intelligencers face each other. There were around thirty men in the room. The intelligencers would be destroyed. At exactly midnight, one minute and thirty seconds, both groups attacked and the tension that used to float in the room disappeared to leave only adrenaline. It was a fight for a life, and it had started.

***

Kyra Einarsson, October 2nd, 2031, 0.01 am

One of the men whom I was fighting finally fell to the floor, breaking his arm at the same time. My heart pounding, I frantically looked around the room. We had merrily walked into a trap and half of our group was now already crawling on the floor, hurt by the overwhelming number of opponents. I ran to one of the intelligencers – I couldn't distinguish who it was in the darkness and the speed of the action – and helped him get rid of his opponent. My legs were dangerously shaking as I suddenly fell on the floor, panting. My opponent lay on me, his weight pressing against my lungs. I nervously looked for my knife in one of my pockets, but the man noticed my frantic moves and stole it before I even had a chance to touch it.

"Itami!" screamed someone.

A warm liquid ran along my cheek, staining my hood. The liquid entered my mouth and the bitter taste of blood spilled on my tongue. I was bleeding and the pain pinching in my body seemed unbearable. My enemy was too strong for me and despite my efforts and proceedings to push him away, he didn't move. The blade of my knife shone over me, and my heartbeats dangerously quickened. I could feel the sadistic glance of my opponent and the gleam in his eyes. He lifted the knife as if it was a game before turning it so it would cut my throat.

"This is your last breath," he whispered in the noise.

I wriggled under him, trying to push him as far as I could. He turned the blade and pointed it at me. His hand rapidly moved towards my heart, quickening as the second passed and I was frozen underneath his grip.

"Itami!" someone shouted again.

The hand of my opponent stopped in the air and the knife sonorously fell on the floor. A dark chain was wrapped around his neck, and he suffocated.

"Go get the papers, Itami, go!" pressed the intelligencer who had saved my life. I briefly nodded and ran to the stairs, stressfully rushing to the ninth floor.

The whole mission was a catastrophe, and it was getting even worse. The whole plan was an ambush; the W.A.F. intelligencers were supposed to have stayed and watched around the building, but they had been trapped as well. Our section drove directly into a bloody trap. The contact between the V.T.S. and us had been cut and we were left alone in the dark building. I finally reached the seventh floor a few minutes later, panting and sweating underneath my hood. I could barely breathe, and the temperature of the building was probably reaching thirty-two degrees. I stopped for a second, shaking, while an orange and yellowish light brightened the floor.

I squinted to see better, briefly forgetting my tiredness and my nervosity. A dark smoke filled up the air of the room, dense and polluted. It spread in the room in few seconds, and I could barely see around me. The smell of fuel hit my senses and I coughed, breathing in the polluted air. The crackling sound produced by the fire got closer and closer. The loud noise covered my coughs as a door burst into ashes in front of me. Suffocating, I crawled to the stairs and escaped as far as I could, blinking in order to see better. Adrenaline drove in my veins and my breaths quickened as I crawled downstairs, forgetting about the papers and the mission.

"Where are you going?" a voice suddenly resounded between the cracks and detonations of the fire, a few floors upon our heads.

I jumped on my feet, detailing a silhouette in the darkness of the office in which we were.

"I thought you were looking for the papers," he said sarcastically. "They're not in the building anyway. We've taken them away before you, silly people, walked in our trap."

I grabbed a tiny metal star that I always kept hidden in my clothes and rapidly threw it at him. He flinched, but gracefully avoided it.

"Is that how you want to solve your problems?" he scornfully asked.

I rapidly jumped backwards and rolled on the ground, grabbing another metallic star. My opponent walked a few steps and stopped in the moonlight so I could see him. Half of his face was covered up with a metallic mask. His hair was long, black, and messy. He wore a long black coat that he slowly took off, simply holding it at the coat hanger behind him. The most frightening thing about him wasn't his impassive calmness or his shiny metallic head. It was his claws. As he took his coat off, his long nails uncoiled to solidify like blades. My heart beats quickened. I had ten sharp enemies.

"Itami, right?" he innocently asked. "How does it feel to experience pain and sufferance every single day?"

"This isn't my real name," I venomously spat.

"Don't you know that the code names in G.U.W.K. are simply reflecting your personality? Your life? Your fate?"

His eyes coldly turned black. Only the light reflected in his eyes, and he calmly said, just like if he had understood everything,

"You are an outlaw, Kyra. You've been banned from our clan."

He rapidly jumped on the desk and one of his nails pierced my shoulder. Blood spilled on my clothes, bursting and staining the office.

"I'm not an outlaw," I articulated with difficulty.

He removed his nails from my shoulder before slowly standing up.

"You are one in our world."

"Which world!?" I shouted, angrily.

"You were banned because you could feel emotions of your own."

"I was never banned!" I replied, not sure about what I was saying.

"Look at your eyes," he simply said.

Shivering, I unwillingly turned my face to the mirror behind me. My eyes were dark, and I could no longer distinguish the pupil from the iris and the whole eyes. Like Dead Claw, only the white reflection of the light was reflected. A cold ran down my back.

"Am I the only one?" I whispered as I turned to face Dead Claw.

"As an outlaw? No, you're not. There are thousands of other failures like you around the world, but no one knows about their existence."

"I'm not a failure!" I screamed.

In a few seconds, I was standing on the desk, holding my dagger in my right hand. A smile stretched Dead Claw's lips.

"Susceptive?"

The atmosphere was electric and the sound of our blades clashing resounded around the room. The temperature in the office increased each second. Soon, the flames appeared in the room and the smoke invaded the air. Dead Claw jumped to the stairs and disappeared in less than a second, leaving me alone on the ground. Squinting, panting, I crawled downstairs, on guard. Dead Claw could be anywhere, and no one knew where I was.

"The game isn't finished!" Dead Claw angrily screamed, pointing his long nails at me.

"Tell me where the papers are!" I cried.

"Never!" he replied.

"Then let us go!" I screamed, but the detonations and the crackling of the wood covered my voice.

"What?"

"Let us go!"

Dead Claw simply sneered.

"I will destroy this damn G.U.W.K system!"

His nails cut my sleeve and another scar formed on my arm.

"You're so weak! I know now why you were banned!"

I threw another star and this time, it tucked into his arm. Dead Claw screamed, irritated.

"You, silly!"

His blade ripped my hood and the black cloth fell on the floor, revealing my face. I gasped and Dead Claw froze. Silence fell around and the tensed atmosphere grew even more unpleasant.

"You..." he simply said.

A wince deformed my face as my dark blood ran down my arms and back.

"What?" I asked, astounded.

He didn't answer but pushed me back and jumped on a chair behind him. I brutally fell on the floor; my breath taken away. His silence was oppressive, and I was frozen, my limbs were sore and the scars on my body dangerously bled. From where I was standing, I couldn't detail his face, but I could see his pursed lips and his chest rising as he breathed. He was panting, just as if he had run the marathon under a burning sun a few minutes earlier. The noise of the fire burning and destroying the building behind us didn't bother the unpleasant silence. For the first time of my life – as far as I could recall – I was scared. I was scared because I didn't know what had happened. I didn't understand what he had understood. Part of my life was still a mystery for me, and I was simply lost.

After several seconds, where I aimlessly tried to escape, crawling down the stairs, he turned to face me, his black eyes shining in an uncertain gleam.

"Do you simply know, how you ended up on Earth, surrounded by thousands of simple humans?" he asked, his voice as cold as ice.

"The governor of our world installed a useful and critical rule, by which none of the aliens able to feel and sense emotions could stay in our clan. These aliens were banished and sent to Earth with nothing but low expectancy to survive. When the governor discovered you, he didn't hesitate any single microsecond to send you on Earth. You've been locked in one of the most dangerous jails for the night when you were only four years old; but in the morning, a surprise awaited our lovely governor; no child was left. Your mom had entered the prison during the night and helped you escape. She sent you to Earth, in a place where, she thought, you would be safe. This rule is still working on today and thousands of children, teenagers or young adults are sent here, as outlaws, because no one wants them in our community."

"So, you've been one of them," I said, trying to control my emotions and the tears running down my cheeks.

He briefly turned, as if I had said something stupid, before answering,

"No."

I frowned.

"I was the governor who created the law."

I froze. The blood stopped in my veins.

"But you see, one of my associates desperately wanted to come to power. After some months, he finally understood that my cruelty was hiding my weakness. I've been tortured for lying and for being one of the 'sensitive aliens'."

"But why did you do this?!" I shouted. "You understand what we feel about being different! Why did you want to banish us?"

"You have to think in the same way as I did at that time," he coldly answered. "Our community would have killed me if they had known earlier."

I stopped, shocked. How could a man do this? How could *someone* do this?

"And then how was G.U.W.K. created? Why was it created? If you've been simply like one of us, you would have lived a normal life!"

"You're so ignorant! There's a paper, a paper containing the code and the information to come back to our world! If I get it, if I touch it, I will be able to go back there! I would be able to show to our world that there's nothing to be afraid of! Who do you think ensured that the door of your prison cell would be open? Who? It was me! Who do you think told your mother how to enter and how to send you away? It was me! And if you're alive right now, it's because I still didn't try to kill you!"

A howl of horror drilled the night. At this very moment, I was shivering. I was shivering and frightened. I understood this howl of injustice coming out from Dead Claw's mouth. I understood his feelings like I'd never done before. His heart was destroyed. And mine too.

"Kyra!" someone shouted.

Tuga appeared at the corner of the wall, holding a long knife in his right hand. Dead Claw turned, the howl disappearing like a cloud of smoke. I didn't have much time to react; the events that followed were blurred in my vision. The pain was numbing me. The flames already licked the furniture in the room.

"NO!"

I heard myself screaming in the building. I jumped in front of Tuga, waving my arms as if to say 'stop, there's nothing we can't do without talking'. But Dead Claw had already checked where he would attack. My eyes twisted on Tuga's black eyes. A twinge drove in my back, and I fell, my mouth opened as if to shout a silent screech.

Chapter 5
Halifax, Nova Scotia, Canada

Kyra Einarsson, October 16th, 2031

Everything around me was white. I could barely distinguish the environment in which I was. Everything seemed so confusing and dazzling. I couldn't hear anything, even though I tried hard. I could barely think. My thoughts seemed to be stuck. Trying to understand what had happened was impossible for me and I lay there, squinting, and blinking in the brightness. I couldn't stir my limbs; they were stuck in a position by a hard plaster keeping them at the right place. My breathing was deep and slow; I had been lying there for a long time.

An almost inaudible hubbub grew in the silence, and I suddenly felt vulnerable. Where was I? The noise grew louder and louder as I frantically tried to move. My memory suddenly came back; in a fraction of second, I remembered everything from A to Z. My life seemed to rapidly pass under my eyes, showing me pictures and images, I barely recalled. A smile, shadows, faces of people I didn't remember. Some movements, some words that came whispering at my ears. The warmth and the coldness of people. The unity and anonymity of some places. The soft and sweet voice of a beautiful mom.

"*If you feel alone, look into the shiny stars, you will see my smile from where you are.*"

A phrase that made sense now. Meeting Dead Claw taught me things I never knew. I was born to be different, born to change the world. But maybe my fate wouldn't change anything after all. Being different was a quality as well as a danger. Being different pushed me to be exiled from my community. My roots, my blood, my personality had me banished.

I squinted and looked at the whiteness upon me. Maybe there, I would see the stars my mom told me about. And the smile; a smile of understanding, hiding an apology, a pity that I could scarcely endure.

"*You know now why you've been banished, right?*" hummed a little voice in my head. "*You know now what you can do to come back, right?*"

I winced, but this cringing little voice didn't stop, no matter how much I wanted to.

"*So, you understand, right? You understand? You understand?*"

Even though I tried, no, I still didn't understand.

The hubbub I heard before resounded in my ears and I straightened my head. I squinted a few times in order to see better, and finally detailed the room in which I was. It was a small, squared room, with no window. The bright light came from the lightbulbs hanging from the roof. The room was cold and empty. The white bed and the nightstand were the only furniture, at one corner. The white door was right in front of me, with a grey lock and no window. My heartbeats quickened. I knew I wasn't in immediate danger, but I became stressed. The hubbub had now stopped in front of my door, and a metallic clatter resounded in the room.

"She's right there," said someone. "Would you wait for me a few seconds?"

"No problem, doctor."

The door opened and a doctor entered the room, holding black clothes in his left hand. When he noticed me, he stopped and smiled.

"You're awake now," he simply said. "Someone's waiting for you outside. Get your hood on."

The black clothes he was holding was a tiny curtain, and he hung it to the ceiling, creating a wall between him and me.

"I... I don't have a cowl," I stuttered.

"On the nightstand."

I looked towards the nightstand, but the doctor had already taken the hood and helped me put it on.

"You've just woken up, right?" he said to himself. "Today is 16th of October, he jotted down in a tiny notebook. How do you feel?"

"Everything hurts," I murmured.

"When Tuga brought you here, to the G.U.W.K.'s hospital, you had many scars on your arms and shoulder, including potentially dangerous ones. You had a terrible scar in the back and had already lost a lot of blood. If Tuga had waited one more minute, we wouldn't have been able to save you," informed the doctor. "You can consider yourself incredibly lucky in your bad luck."

"And the others? The mission?" I asked, my heartbeats quickening.

"Dead Claw has been arrested and is now locked in a prison cell. The others were saved, and everyone survived, however with many injuries. What you did in the building is totally unknown, but what the G.U.W.K. governor knows, it's that the mission failed one more time. However, with Dead Claw under arrest, it is still possible to achieve it, and he still hasn't fired any of you."

He still hasn't fired any of you. Great information. He could fire me; I would be more than happy. But that was another story.

"Dead Claw shouldn't be under arrest," I said.

The doctor looked at me.

"Sorry?"

"Dead Claw shouldn't be under arrest," I repeated.

The doctor put down his notebook and his pen on the nightstand and cleaned his glasses before looking at me once again.

"He has committed several crimes, don't you know?"

"I know. But you should give him a second chance. Let him go. He has what he needs. You're the only ones blocking his path. I'm sure that if you let him back to freedom, he will disappear, and you will never hear of him anymore."

"How can you be sure? Do you know things you didn't tell us? Is there anything important that happened that night?"

"No, nothing," I lied. "But my instinct tells me to do this."

The doctor raised his eyebrows.

"An instinct is worth nothing against facts."

I sighed. I should have known the conversation would end like this. It was obvious. The doctor cleared his voice before saying,

"Someone is waiting for you outside. Put your hood on. I will rewrite this information on computer."

He showed me the notebook.

"Have a good afternoon."

He left without saying anything else.

The door opened and closed behind him. I heard some voices coming from the corridor and the door slowly opened again.

"Itami?" a shy voice said.

"Tuga?" I replied.

The young man walked past the curtain and appeared by my side. His black cowl covered his face and he slowly sat on my bed.

"Are you fine?"

"Could be better," I answered.

The atmosphere was awkward, and I didn't know what to do. Tuga was sitting next to me, and we were both trying to avoid each other's eyes.

"Hum…" he said. "Thank you for saving my life."

"I didn't save you," I replied. "I made sure Dead Claw wouldn't make a mistake he would regret."

"Something he would regret? He wouldn't regret anything. He's a murderer." I didn't say anything and looked at the white wall on my left side.

"Sorry," he whispered. "He has been locked in one of the hospital's rooms, maybe you will be able to go and talk to him," he sighed.

His left hand grabbed his hood, and he would have taken it off if I hadn't stopped him.

"No!" I shouted. "We can't see each other's faces. Our identity must be kept secret."

A couple of seconds passed.

"You know... I don't really care about the rules anymore. I have had enough of G.U.W.K.; I'm fed up. I will quit as soon as I can."

"You can't," I said.

I knew it was impossible to quit G.U.W.K., to have checked many times in the official papers concerning the organisation. He didn't look up and I suddenly understood.

"You can't do that!"

"There's a meeting in thirty minutes about the mission," he informed, totally ignoring what I had said.

"I'm coming."

"No, you're not. I will tell you what we will have discussed."

He stood up and walked to the curtain.

"I have to go now, I'll come back after. Get better soon."

He turned and I heard the door opening and closing before the silence invaded the room again.

A nurse came forty-five minutes later with a wheelchair and clean clothes. She smiled and spoke to me while I was getting ready. She had long black hair and a friendly smile. She seemed kind and nice and seeing her helped me forget about the meeting I was missing. She helped me sit in the wheelchair; my arms and shoulders were covered with bandaging and so was my body. I could barely move. The pain in my bones was horrifying and almost unbearable. The nurse noticed it and she gave me a powerful medicine. She opened the door of my room and pushed me in the corridor, talking about everything and nothing at the same time.

The typical smell of hospitals aggressed me as soon as we entered the corridor. On the left, a few doctors and nurses wearing green or white coats were rushing about, holding important papers or medical instruments. Surgeons were chatting about an important surgery. On the right, the long corridor was endlessly stretching, lit by the neon on the ceiling. People were coughing, sneezing, shivering under warm blankets. The in-flight meals were still next to the patient's beds.

The nurse pushed me into a special room where other doctors were already setting things up. She helped me to sit on the bed in the middle of the room as one of the doctors turned to face me. They changed my bandages and I finally saw the long scars stretching on my arms, shoulders and to my back. I stood on my feet for the first time in two weeks. The nurse was especially nice with me and helped me. My arm around her shoulders, I walked around the room, testing the senses like I had not done in a long time. For the first time in my life, I realised how much the senses were crucial. I felt as if a burden had been taken off my shoulders. I could smell, see, hear, taste, sense. The nurse gave me crutches and I grabbed them.

As soon as the nurse guided me back into my room and turned to visit other patients, I grabbed my crutches and, limping, walked to the entrance hall of the hospital. The receptionist welcomed me with a bright smile, asking,

"How can I help you?"

"I would like to see one of the intelligencers sent to Havana two weeks ago…"

"Yes, let me see…"

She grabbed a book and put it on the counter, looking through the last pages.

"Do you remember the name?" I heard her ask.

But I was already gone.

I limped to the elevator and pressed the cold button. The orange light brightened for a few seconds and the metallic doors opened. People walked out and I entered with a few visitors and nurses. One of the nurses pressed the 4th button and the doors closed. The elevator slowly moved up the hospital with no noise. We stopped at the first and second floor before moving on to the fourth floor. The nurse disappeared in one of the corridors, leaving me alone in front of the elevator. I checked the room numbers and staggered to one of the white doors at the far end of the white corridor. There was no noise to be heard here, only the distant clatter of medical activities. I stopped in front of the last door and pressed the doorknob. The door didn't open. I silently sighed.

I knew that I should help him, but how? The door was closed, I was carrying crutches and I had absolutely no idea how I should help Dead Claw. I quietly put my hand on the door. It was cold and empty. There was no history between these walls, just solid construction materials. I turned my head and looked at the window on my left.

"Dead Claw?" I murmured at the door.

I didn't have to wait long for an answer.

"Itami?"

"Do you have a window in your room?"

"It's locked and there are bars."

I turned to face the corridor. A nurse was coming in my direction. She stopped by the door and took the key out of her pocket, smiling to me.

"Do you need anything?" she asked.

"No, I'm fine, thank you."

She turned and unlocked the door.

"Can you please tell me where room six hundred fifty-two is? I forgot where it was."

She stopped and walked towards me. She walked a bit with me, her hand on my shoulder. She was close enough to me. If I could reach the keys...

"The elevator is at the end of the corridor, you go to the second floor and other nurses will help you find your way," she said.

I smiled back and walked to the elevator. She turned, facing the wall on her left, and walked to the closed door. She hadn't noticed her bunch of keys was missing.

Once back in my room, seven minutes later, I sat on my bed, hiding an impish smile. I hopped to the sink and removed my cowl to wash my face. The cold water ran down my cheekbones and nose, forming water droplets on my chin. They fell one by one, creating a rhythm in agreement with the slowed down seconds. I wiped my face and threaded my hood as the door opened in a sudden crash. Tuga entered, informing and shouting,

"Dead Claw escaped! Itami, get ready!"

"Hang on a minute!" cut in a man at the door of my room. "You've made enough mistakes. The mission will be given to other intelligencers. In addition, Miss Itami is not able to solve any mission for the moment. I order you to stay as far away from this dilemma as possible. Once Dead Claw will be found, I will see what I will do with the intelligencers responsible for the failure of mission 337!"

The leader of G.U.W.K. disappeared, leaving us alone in my hospital room. Tuga sat in silence on my bed, and I kept standing, not knowing if I should jump with happiness or sit and cry.

"You didn't help Dead Claw to escape, right?" Tuga suddenly asked.

"I can barely walk," I answered. "And I don't even know where his room is."

Tuga raised his eyebrows but didn't ask any other questions about Dead Claw's escape. We both sat in the room, looking at an invisible point on the black curtain miserably hanging from the ceiling.

"There will be a ball tomorrow evening," suddenly informed Tuga. "Would you like to come with me?"

I glanced at him, agreeably surprised.

"With great pleasure," I answered, smiling. "But we'll be fired before it," I added, laughing.

Indeed, there was no chance for us to stay in the intelligence unit.

***

Kyra Einarsson, October 18th, 2031

"Kyra, you scared us," complained Callie.

I was sitting in the café in front of Nathaniel and Callie, at the exact same place as last time. The empty coffee and teacups gathered in the centre of the table and I was trying to calm Nathaniel and Callie down after my two friends had jumped to hug me.

"I am sincerely sorry," was the only thing I found to say.

"Sincerely sorry? Sincerely sorry?" repeated Callie.

"Callie," interrupted Nathaniel. "Don't make things worse."

Callie stopped and pursed her lips, despite her will to talk and reprimand me.

"Where's Loven?" I asked, even though I probably knew the answer.

"He got a new job in the city; you know he's working in the shop at the corner of the street. He couldn't come," responded Nathaniel.

"Well, he could have come," replied Callie. "He told me he was starting at four o'clock; it's half past three."

"It doesn't really matter."

A long silence followed.

"Have you heard about the dangerous criminal's escape?" asked Nathaniel suddenly. He's apparently wandering around Halifax at this very moment. The police have been chasing him for a long time, and they arrested him in Havana, around two weeks ago. But he managed to escape from the hospital room in which he was locked."

"Yeah, I've heard about it," I simply answered.

The afternoon was long and when I finally stopped in front of my house at around five o'clock, I felt like if I was back home. The garden was clean. The two cars were parked in the garage. The windows lit the street from a yellow light. Beverly had lowered the curtains, but I could still see their silhouettes moving around. Elias was talking to Rachel. Beverly was walking from the kitchen to the dining room, holding dishes in her hands. I didn't know if Mandy was back, but I didn't hesitate one more second and ran to the entry door. I frantically rang at the door. I heard the movement stop in the house. The few paces Elias made to walk to the white door. The lock as Elias turned it to the right to open. His smile when he finally saw me.

"Kyra!" he said.

I jumped in his arms as my two sisters appeared in the tiny entry hall.

"Kyra, you're back!" Beverly and Rachel said.

"Oh, my dear!" said Mandy, running to hug me as well. "Elias received a letter, he told me you were in hospital, but we weren't allowed to visit you!"

I turned to face Elias. He was probably one of the only people I trusted the most on Earth. He smiled again and we walked to the dining room, discussing, and chatting about the latest gossip.

***

Elias Einarsson, October 18th, 2031

I was pleasantly surprised when I noticed Kyra standing on the steps. I didn't expect seeing her before a long time. I was the only one in the family who knew about the existence of G.U.W.K. and Kyra's role in it. I was the only one who really knew everything about Kyra, and I would never say anything to anyone. When I walked into her room that evening, I knew she would tell me something important; and so, she did.

"Kyra?" I asked at the door.

"Elias," she answered, sitting in her office chair.

"How was the mission? I've read many things in the newspapers, but I bet they aren't completely true."

"I've learnt there are others like me," she simply told me.

I looked at her for a few seconds.

"That's great."

"You knew it would end like this, right?" she asked. "Your dream came true. Maybe one day, you will be able to show the world that there are not only humans. But that we live next to them every single day since their birth".

"I won't say anything, Kyra. I learnt a lot. I learnt that you had feelings. You're not just a random newspaper article that everyone laughs at when they read it. I know now that I was right. But convincing others would be a waste of time. Now, I can consider the future, maybe find a way to live on Mars, or maybe Europe? And I don't talk about our Europe, on Earth…"

I smiled. A smile of sadness.

"I knew one day you would leave us."

"I have understood many things in a few days," she said. "I know the cure for my heartache."

"Then if you know it, you could stay with us," I replied, with a gleam of hope shining in my eyes.

The lamp in the corner of the room flashed and darkness briefly invaded the room. Our breath was the only sound. The seconds were long. The light came back in the room, and I looked at Kyra.

"If you feel alone, look into the shiny stars, you will see my smile from where you are," she said.

I didn't reply but stood up. Kyra jumped on her feet, and she hugged me, wiping the tears running down her cheeks.

***

Chapter 6
Halifax, Nova Scotia, Canada

Kyra Einarsson, October 19th, 2031

I briefly smiled to Loven as I walked passed in front of him. I had entered the little shop two minutes earlier, even though I had nothing to buy inside. I however bought a tiny bottle of water that I quickly paid, before waving to Loven, almost shouting a 'goodbye', he probably didn't hear. I had written all the steps I would make in the next two days and the first one was almost achieved. I had said adieu to Mandy, Beverly, Rachel and Elias and it was now turn for Callie and Nathaniel. My skateboard under my arm, I walked to the street before jumping on it and heading to Callie's house. My heart was beating as fast as a machine gun and the cold driving in my veins had already made me shiver a few times.

"Kyra!" Callie said as she opened the door, a few minutes later.

I stopped in front of her as she looked at me.

"Don't you want to come in?"

"No," I said.

Callie frowned. I knew I wouldn't find the words I needed to speak and so I gave her the letter I had written.

"Bye," I simply said.

She grabbed the letter and by the time she had read her name, I was gone.

When the clocks showed 4 pm, I was sitting in the same hospital as where I had stayed after the failed mission. My heart deliberately hurt, but I tried to ignore the pain driving in my veins. It was incredibly hard to forget how hard everything would be from now on and how I would have to fight for what I thought was right.

The room in which I was waiting was cold and white. It was smaller than the last one, but still big enough to welcome a few visitors. The bed was relatively comfortable, lit by the window on the left. A black backpack stood by my side, already open. A black dress laid on the bed, soft and beautiful. I swallowed with difficulty. Not for the dress, not for the party tonight; but for Elias. He was the one who was ready to believe in me, whatever path I chose to follow.

Next to the dress was a mask; a simple dark mask covered with shiny diamonds. A masked ball took place on that night, or, in other words, a masked party. And as far as I understood the leader of G.U.W.K., it was my last one. The doctor came later than he should have and took my bandages off. He checked some important information, gave me the results, and disappeared once again, leaving me alone in the room. I quickly changed clothes to wear my dress, grabbed my schoolbag and my mask and left the hospital, heading for the G.U.W.K.'s headquarters.

***

The room in which the party was taking place, including a short speech and a few thanks to the intelligencers, was huge. No other words could describe the size of the hall. The ceiling was incredibly high, the chandeliers were grand and shiny, the red carpet on the floor covered half of the endless rectangular room and the white tablecloth covered the long buffet tables. Waiters and waitresses walked around the room holding salvers full of flutes of champagne. The tall, narrow glasses didn't last for long on the plateau the waiters were holding. Intelligencers from different sections of the system chatted and discussed things around the room about the newest gossip. All wore masks, which covered half of their faces. When I entered the huge room with huge windows, I stopped. The view was breath-taking and astounding. All details seemed to be perfectly detailed, all tiny issues were solved by clever ideas and the time was slowing down.

"Good evening," someone welcomed me.

I turned to face the leader. He simply smiled, before shaking hands.

"I hope you'll enjoy the masked party," he said.

"Certainly."

He briefly looked at me with his dark and shiny eyes before saying,

"We should probably go to the balcony for a few minutes. I have important things to talk about with you."

I was too tired to protest and followed him until the tiny balcony at the opposite end of the room. When we stepped outside, he rapidly closed the door behind us and turned to face me; his dark eyes detailing me. The darkness outside made it harder for us to see each other.

"I've been strict and heavy-handed during the last missions, and I think I expected too much from you, didn't I?" he started. "As the leader of G.U.W.K., I have to pay attention to each and every one of my intelligencers," he continued. "I know them better than everyone else. I sometimes know them better than themselves. And I can tell that you were one of the easiest and the hardest to understand."

I held my breath. He had completely caught my attention.

"You entered here young compared to the others. But compared to some others, your stay in the system will be shortened. You helped a lot, Itami, during all the missions. And even if many of our intelligencers died in Cuba, even if we didn't find the papers, you're still one of the greatest intelligencers I have ever had."

He looked me in the eyes, holding two flutes of champagne he had taken from a waiter when we were still inside. He gave me one, took a sip and continued,

"You know what the papers are for, right?"

I nodded.

"It contains a code and information," I answered, not knowing if I should say more or not.

"It contains a code and information on how to go back to our world," he completed. "Itami, G.U.W.K. stands for Galaxy's Universal Worth Kids. All of us, here, in this system, are part of the same world. A world that lives far away from us, maybe in the stars, maybe in another planet, maybe in another milky way. We're *brothers and sisters*, Itami. We're here for the same reason as you are."

"You mean that... You mean that..." I pointed at the doors, looked at him, looked at the doors again.

"We're all extra-terrestrial living organisms, banished on Earth because difference isn't accepted where we lived, he completed. We are all equal, despite our differences. But there's always a time when I have to let my intelligencers go."

I frowned when he looked at me in the eyes.

"I'll let you go as soon as the masked party will end," he informed. "And you will have the time to do whatever you want to. I know you have problems to solve. I hope that you will change the world into a better place."

"My sacrifice might change our world, and make it accept differences," I finished.

We both smiled, a shy, simple smile and I understood the conversation had ended. I walked to the doors and pressed the doorknob when a voice interrupted my move,

"One more thing, Itami!" the leader said. "You probably know that Itami has a meaning, right?" he hesitated.

"I know, but never tried to check mine."

"It means pain."

He looked away for a few seconds.

"You've got the 'M' sign in your left hand. You will accomplish a lot of things, even if it will be through pain."

I automatically looked at the palm of my left hand. For the first time of my life since I couldn't remember, a smile stretched my lips. A real big smile full of emotions. The sign was there, in the palm of my hand. The lines were deep and perfectly drawn. Whatever it would take.

"Goodbye, sir," I answered, before leaving the balcony.

***

When I entered the room again, a hubbub welcomed me. The dancefloor in the corner of the room was crowded, the buffet tables were almost empty, and more and more people chatted all around about different things. I looked for Tuga, who I was supposed to spend the party with, but couldn't find him. I walked between the cluster of people, tiptoeing between the tables, the waiters, and the intelligencers. Suddenly, I stopped, agape. Tuga stood in front of me, a few meters away, in a dark suit fitting him perfectly. His eyes met mine, and an electrical thrill spilled in my heart. We slowly walked towards each other, an imaginary silence encircling us.

"Good evening," we both said as we stopped in front of each other.

We smiled and briefly looked away, nervous. His perfume surrounded me and I recognised the magic chemicals moving between us, the warmth in his arms, the smile on his face. But where did I know it from?

"You look gorgeous," he said.

"Thanks."

I looked away, feeling awkward.

"Do you want to dance?" I asked.

A song had started playing in the room and couples wearing their party masks started dancing on the dancefloor.

"Of course."

My heartbeats quickened and I sighed, happy that he had answered positively. We walked to the dancefloor and started dancing according to the music and the rhythm.

The melody seemed bewitching and unreal. As we started dancing, we flew to another world, a world hidden to anyone else. We were dancing on soft clouds, breathing in a pure and imaginary world. A pure and imaginary world where none of the true sadness could reach us and stain our hopes. Because in a certain way, we were still kids. The beauty of childhood still lived in us. Its flame was dying, dying with age, dying with everything. But the gleam, the glimmer was still there, hidden between the debris of misery.

I slowly spun on the dancefloor as the music stopped. Tuga smiled and I returned his grin. The notes continued playing and we started again, dancing between the other masked couples. A fresh breeze came from the open doors leading to the balcony, at the other end of the room. It was calm and peaceful.

"Shall we go outside?" asked Tuga. "It's really hot in this room…"

I agreed and we walked to the balcony. The night had fallen on the city and the distant lights of the city shone like bright stars. A soft breeze caressed our skin as we admired the view. Trees and plants grew huge shadows on the ground, while the city centre's skyscrapers overhung the parks and residential areas. On my left, I could distinguish the familiar silhouette of houses behind the squared ones of condos. A few cars still drove around the city; their headlights sparkling as they drove pass bare maple trees.

"It's outstanding here," I said, speechless.

"The decorations for Halloween are nice, too," Tuga added.

I turned to face him, smiling.

"Are only the decorations nice?"

"No. You're nice too."

I probably blushed as my heart pinched.

"I love you," I whispered underneath my breath.

My heartbeats quickened dangerously as I nervously tried to find something to look at instead of stupidly standing in front of him. But sadly, I didn't know where to look and I could only meet his eyes shining in the dark. An unpleasant silence followed my precipitated words. I should probably have thought more carefully before quickly telling what I had to say. It probably wasn't the correct time nor place to say something so serious.

"Well, I understand that…" I tried to say.

I could hear the melody of the music from where I was.

"That…" I hesitated.

And I could smell his perfume, blown by the breeze in my direction.

"It might not be reciprocal," I quickly finished.

I walked to the hall where the party was still ongoing and left the meeting, briefly waving at the leader of the G.U.W.K. system. I grabbed my coat and ran outside, taking my mask off. One tear menaced falling down my cheek as I walked on the passageway. The streetlamps were the only source of light in the night. I didn't notice where I was going; I was just following my steps, wandering around the city in the cold night. My breath turned into white smoke as it touched the cold temperature. My nose froze, my cheekbones turned pinkish.

"Wait!" called someone behind me.

I stopped and turned, curious.

Tuga's face was only a few centimetres away from mine, still hidden by his mask. He frowned, holding his grip on my right arm.

My mask.

I had taken my mask off. The streetlamp behind him didn't allow me to see his face, but he could clearly detail mine.

"Kyra?" he asked.

I frowned.

"How do you know me?" I asked, bitterly.

If he wanted to say something like 'I'm sorry', I was not sure to be able to contain my anger. But instead of answering anything silly, or instead of talking, he simply took his mask off. His move was slow and long. It seemed to last for hours. He grabbed it with the pulp of his fingers. Took it off. Revealed his face. I froze, shocked.

"Kyra, sincerely…"

I shook my head from left to right, unable to say anything.

"Kyra, sincerely…" he tried again.

I shook my head again, looking away. How could this be true? The warmth of his arms. The magic chemicals moving between us. I remembered now. I remembered from where I already knew him. My tears freezing on my cheeks. He pulled me closer, hugging me for the second time.

"If I had known it was you before…" I said.

"Yes, but you didn't know, Kyra," he said.

He grabbed my chin and lifted it so I would look into his eyes.

"I am really sorry for the things I told you that night," I apologized. "I loved Tuga, how could I have known it was you?"

"It's alright. Tuga and Loven are one person. And so are Kyra and Itami."

A few seconds passed.

"So, you know now why our hearts hurt, right? Especially when we are close to the person we love?"

"Because love is forbidden. That's why we were banished."

"But I'll never stop loving you," he whispered to my ear.

I looked at him in the eyes.

"So, this is all we can do now, right?"

It was difficult to admit. It was difficult to imagine.

"I guess so," he answered.

"Remember that I will always love you, no matter how far I am, no matter how hard it is," I murmured against his chest.

Epilogue

Dead Claw had found Kyra on October 20th, 2031, at 1 am in the morning. She was alone, in the middle of the street, weeping underneath her large hood. He carried the papers. The papers containing the code and the information on how to go back to their world. And he did something that, he thought, he would have never done. They left together. They went back to the world where they used to live; the world where they were born.

As the minutes passed, Kyra's immune system started destroying its own cells. A disease with which she had lived all her life. As the hours passed, her situation got worse. She could barely stand and walk; she was crawling, panting, and drooling. He hoped he would be able to rescue her. He was ready to do anything. She had saved his life even if she didn't have to. He wanted to help her. Just help her. Because he felt guilty about all the things he had done before.

But as the seconds passed, he knew he wouldn't be able to do anything. He was standing in the corner of the room. Another man was by his side, holding a gun. He was there, frozen, quiet. He heard her plea; he heard her murmuring 'help me...'. But he was just frozen. The other man was the leader of their world. When they came back, they realised that nothing had changed.

"Leave her alone! He heard himself say. She has the right to decide by herself."

Then, he froze. Kyra suffered. The man held the gun. He started a countdown. And he, couldn't stir from where he was.

But suddenly, Kyra seemed to become absent. She seemed to think. She seemed to live in another world. He watched her on the ground. She was beautiful. Beautiful in a particular way. She had lived things that other people had never experienced. She stood and looked straight until the very last moment. She fought for the things she believed were right.

Suddenly, she stirred again, tried to reach Dead Claw. The other man didn't know what to do. He had stopped counting and his gun was simply pointing at the ground at his feet.

"Please."

Dead Claw kneeled by her side. He put his hand on her shoulder. It was mechanical. He might not feel like helping. Maybe he just didn't remember how to help someone.

"Get out of here!" screamed the other man. "I will shoot her!"

Dead Claw turned to face him. He met his eyes. Cold. Distant. Not even the simplest form of warmth. This man was just like he used to be. He had also been a horrible leader.

Kyra glanced at Dead Claw through her tears which blurred her vision. She also briefly looked at the other man. If they had both thought that it would be a great idea, to come back into this world to make a change, they now realised how wrong they had been. They hadn't seen many people before being locked in this horrifyingly white room and they were now stuck with a sadistic leader about to kill them.

"You should never have come back!" screamed the angry man.

Dead Claw turned his face to detail Kyra's eyes.

"Maybe that's true," he articulated with difficulty.

"It's wrong," Kyra stuttered. "Even if we did a little, maybe one day, it will change."

She joined her hands together under Dead Claw's careful eyes.

"To all the people that I trust and love and that I can count on my fingers. Elias, Mandy, Beverly, Rachel, Callie, Nathaniel, Loven. And even you, Dead Claw. Because I don't feel like being mad at anyone right now."

She gathered a bit of energy, a bit, but enough to let her stand on her feet under Dead Claw's surprised eyes. How could she feel better?

"Stop these ridiculous, endless speeches!" screamed the man's hoarse voice.

He pulled the trigger and a sudden detonation exploded. The walls dangerously vibrated. A thrill roamed around the room. The buzz of the lightbulbs seemed to be the only sign of life. Despite the man's jerky's breath. A puddle of cardinal red spilled on the white-washed floor. A smile stretched the man's lips. He had killed two birds with one stone. He killed two enemies with one bullet. He smirked and left the room.

In Kyra's open eyes, the star had disappeared, leaving only a dark sight where the pupil and the iris weren't distinct anymore. They were just open eyes looking towards the ceiling. Towards the sky.

If you feel alone, look into the shiny stars, you will see my smile from where you are.

That's what she did.

***